HEARTLAND

HEARTLAND

JOHN OMWAKE

Copyright © 2015 by John Omwake

ISBN 978-1-4958-0642-1
ISBN 978-1-4958-0643-8 eBook

Published April 2015

INFINITY PUBLISHING
1094 New DeHaven Street, Suite 100
West Conshohocken, PA 19428-2713
Toll-free (877) BUY BOOK
Local Phone (610) 941-9999
Fax (610) 941-9959
Info@buybooksontheweb.com
www.buybooksontheweb.com

The Stories

Alone

He was an old man who had lived all the years he wanted. His back ached. Legs and feet once agile were now stiff, arthritis gnarled fingers once nimble. All he could do was sit in a rocking chair and gaze at the mountain on the far side of the lake. At its top was a formation that resembled a kettle turned upside down. Early settlers dubbed it Kettle Mountain. The handle stuck.

It was a mountain guests liked to climb. The old man was one of them. Each summer for years he had climbed it. For much of the way the ascent was mild, but when you reached the foot of the inverted kettle it became vertical. If you didn't watch your step you could trip, tumble down mountain. The old man had done this. He never hurt himself badly: a scraped shin, a bruised ankle. Others weren't so lucky. One if not careful could break a limb. One if not careful could die; so far none had. This was a mountain to be taken seriously.

His climbing days were over. Now he sat and gazed. That was better than nothing and for him nothing was not being here in August. That day would come. "This could be my last year," he said to Kate, the pleasant girl at the

1

front desk, as she welcomed him back. "It's getting too hard for me."

She said she hoped that wasn't so. He hoped so too. But he could no longer stand the driving. When he began coming, the trip from Fort Myers was done in two days. Now it took three with frequent stops. And still his back gave trouble. But being here made the pain tolerable, for this year anyway. As for next year he would wait and see.

This was the first year he had come by himself. Over winter his wife of fiftyseven years gave up the ghost. He buried her and worked through his grief, sold their house and removed to a retirement home. It was the smart thing to do, but he didn't like it. He was lonelier there than he had been in the house with its familiar furniture and smells. He could hardly wait to be here. And now he was.

Voices, faces greeted him: pleasant Kate at the front desk, Vonnie the hostess in the dining hall, Luann who served him. All were happy to see him, all were sorry about his wife, all wished him an enjoyable stay. They were better friends than anyone in the retirement home. There he had no friends. Here he did.

Familiar too were the surroundings. But this year things were not the same. He was given his usual table, next to a window with a view of Kettle Mountain. But the table was for two and only he sat at it. Each night Luann brought his Scotch and water. But no gin and tonic for his wife. She was back in Florida, her ashes inurned in the Episcopal church where they worshiped. He was alone and he knew not what to do.

At a nearby table sat a man, younger, fifties perhaps. He was by himself and seemed not to mind. Indeed he acted as though it was the most natural thing to do. This the old man could not fathom. No one by himself could be content. One night at dinner he rose from his chair, walked to the younger man's table.

"Please excuse me," he said, "but I see you're by yourself."

The younger man said he was.

"I don't know how you do it."

The younger man did not understand.

"I lost my wife last winter. Since then I've been by myself and it's the worst feeling I've ever had. I can't stand it and I don't know how you can."

The younger man said he had always sat alone in restaurants, saw nothing strange about that.

"But are you happy?"

The younger man supposed he was: it all he'd ever known and he had found ways to live with it.

The old man returned to his table more confused than before. He could not be like this younger man: alone, pretending to be happy. He had to be with someone else. That was how he had lived for fiftyseven years. Now he had to learn to be by himself. He doubted if he could.

His marriage had been a good one, mostly. They'd met while at university. He was pursuing a doctorate in chemistry. She was still an undergraduate, a student of French. They did not marry until both were graduated and he had a job with a global chemicals conglomerate. It took years for them to settle down. His company had spotted him as a coming man, sent him to places around the world. She went with him and made as good a home as she could during brief stays here and there.

Along the way she bore a son. At an early age it was clear he would not grow up in his father's image. His mind was turned to music. He loved to play it, loved to write it. While still a boy he began to compose musical scores. By the time he was at conservatory his work was performed by others, even got notices on the arts pages of newspapers. Great things were predicted for him.

But at twentyfour years of age he began to experience headaches. Doctors examined him, found tumors on his brain. There was nothing they could do. The world of music mourned a genius whose promise would never be fulfilled. His parents mourned a son. A genius could be replaced, a son could not.

They still had each other. After the time in married life when many couples slept apart they shared a bed. They did things together. Each year without fail they came here, always during the same two weeks in August. He climbed Kettle Mountain while she sat on the terrace, tracking in her mind his progress to the summit, then down again. Upon his return she kissed him, privately sighing in relief that no harm had come his way.

Now she was gone. Now in addition to no son he had no wife. Now he was an old man with afflictions common to old men. Now he had to be happy with a rocking chair, gazing at the mountain he had once scaled, envisioning people climbing up and down. Only in his mind could he climb with them.

He wanted to climb that mountain, taste again the thrill of standing at its summit, look out at mountains rolling into the distance, picture the cities that lay beyond. Look down also, at the main building ringed by cabins no larger than Monopoly houses. At the lake that seemed only a puddle, at the trees. One was the tallest of its kind in the world but to him, a splinter. See all this, and rejoice. He wanted to climb Kettle Mountain, gaze from its summit one last time.

●

He had got a good night's rest. Like other men of his years he got up in the middle of the night, but after doing his business he soon fell asleep. When he awoke he felt more alive than he had in years.

He would start out after breakfast. The climb took two hours, the descent somewhat less. But he needed more time. He reckoned on five hours, total. He would pause to rest and, refreshed, resume climbing until he was tired again. That way he might reach the summit.

The day was Sunday. In years past he and his wife walked to the little church across the highway to receive communion. Neither had grown up religious, but after their son died they thirsted for God. An Episcopal priest showed where to find him. They had grown devout. The old man felt badly, not being in church. But climbing Kettle Mountain one last time was more important.

For a time he sat in the lobby, let his breakfast settle. Then he visited the men's room and saw to his needs. That done he jammed his beatup golf hat on his head, grabbed his walking stick. It was a plain crooked stick he had bought thirty years before, after he had slipped while coming down from the summit, skinning his legs. He would not do that now, would have his stick firmly in hand. Lastly he scooped a plastic bottle of water from a barrel and paid for it at the front desk. Kate took his money. She asked what his plans were.

"I'm going for a walk," he said.

"But you always go to church on Sunday."

"I've decided to go for a walk instead."

She wished him an enjoyable walk. The old man smiled. He liked Kate. If he told her he was climbing Kettle Mountain she might fret. So he said nothing more.

●

To reach the trail up Kettle Mountain he had to descend a row of steps leading to a narrow bridge spanning a stream. Gingerly he negotiated the steps, taking care not to trip himself. Before tackling the bridge he paused. To the left of the pathway was a dam that had been built eighty years earlier to store water for the lake. On the bank was a gazebo with some seats. He took one of them.

During the very long while he had been coming here hardly anything had changed. This was a place where tradition was honored. Jacket and tie were required for men at dinner. Sunday lunch was always fried chicken. Saturday dinner was steak; on Wednesday it was roast beef. Entertainment after dinner was bingo, horse racing, a movie, a lecture perhaps: never anything fancy. Some guests made foursomes for a game of bridge. Others retired to the terrace where they sat until darkness fell. Entertainment ceased between nine thirty and ten, bridge parties broke up, guests walked upstairs to their rooms or across the lawn to their cabins. All was still until seven in the morning, when the dining hall opened for breakfast. Guestrooms were plain: no telephones, no television, no air conditioning, thin walls of knotty pine, handcrafted furniture bearing marks of use and of time, bathroom fixtures that worked when the mood struck. Years before, someone had quipped that this was summer camp for adults. The old man saw truth in that. It reminded him of the camp he had attended as a boy: the spartan rooms, the bell out front that summoned all to meals, the huge dining hall with long rows of tables in the middle. It was all that, yet people who could afford Sea Island or White Sulphur Springs came here because they liked it. It was predictable, comfortable: an unchanging place in a changing world—

It was time to move on. Planting his stick firmly on the ground, he got up from his seat, pivoted his weight on the stick. Though he was not a heavy man the bridge swayed under his weight. He took his time to cross to the other side where the trails began. Each had a sign with its name on it, pointing to where one should go. The old man looked for the sign that read Kettle Mountain. When he saw it he began climbing.

It was a narrow path, beaten down by decades of climbers. In places grass had grown over it. Here and there other trails branched off. If he did not watch where he was going he could get lost. He knew the way, even after years of not walking it, but he had to be careful.

Soon he saw a large log alongside the trail and decided to rest. This time his thoughts did not wander, remained fixed on the present: not as good a time, the worst time. His wife was recently gone, his son long gone; now he was alone, sitting on a log by a trail. He could die on this mountain and nobody would know. Vonnie and Luann would wonder why he didn't show up for dinner. Kate would wonder also. They would ask themselves questions, then ask others. People would be sent to find him. But they would not know where to look.

And if he didn't come back? It would not be bad. Reach the summit and die, looking out at mountains as far as the eye could see. It would not be bad at all.

He sat on the log until he reckoned he could resume. The grade got steeper, his breath shorter. The higher he climbed the stops grew more frequent, lasted longer. It would take all day to reach the summit. But he would not quit.

Dogs and cats came to mind. When they got old and infirm they went off to a place only they knew. There they died. Perhaps their owners would find their carcasses, perhaps not. It didn't matter. They went off, alone, to die. It was what they wanted to do.

Was he doing the same? Was he, like an old dog, going off to die? Was this what he wanted to do? Yes. He wanted a place where he could die alone and in peace. He had seen his day: one that had lasted too long.

He was born in Prague, brought to the new world as an infant. His parents were German speaking Jews: educated and cultured folk who upon reaching these shores traded their names for new ones, their religion for none. They became sufficiently well off to provide their only child with piano and violin lessons, the best album for his stamps, the best clothes and, more importantly, a first rate education. They gave him everything, it seemed, but the thing he craved most: love. He was reared without siblings or religion or affection: a lonely agnostic in an outgoing and religious land.

He was different. He knew. His parents could shed names and faith, they could not shed accents. They took care to see that he grew speaking without a trace of accent, but people hearing them speak knew he was from another land. It set him apart, made him lonelier still.

Only after marrying a woman from a background different from his—brothers and sisters, a warm and loving family—did he begin not to feel alone. He resented his parents for bringing him up as a lonely boy. When they died he buried and then forgot about them. He had come into a new life, a good life. On the day he married he swore that never again, so long as he should live, would he be alone.

But now he was alone: truly and unalterably alone. He had no family, few friends (most were now dead), no hope. He was alone in a world with no further use for him. He had no further use for that world. The sooner he left it the better.

That was why he was climbing Kettle Mountain. Why like a dog he chose to go off to die. Why he decided not to go to church. He would leave this world as he had come into it: a human apart.

●

In front of and above him loomed the formation that gave the mountain its name. He paused for a sip of water, took a handkerchief from his pocket and mopped his brow. The band of his hat was soaked in sweat. He took it off, eyed the sweat, then crushed it back on his head. Pieces of rock jutted up. He was careful not to trip on one of them. He had walked this trail many times, remembered every step. It could have been yesterday when he last climbed Kettle Mountain. But it had been years, ever since his back began troubling him. It troubled him now. The pain was so intense he wondered if he could take another step. But he did. His chest tightened, he gasped for breath: warnings to stop, warnings he ignored.

From within a voice spoke, telling him to go on, look out one last time over those mountains. The voice spoke, he walked. He was walking to his destruction, but no matter. He welcomed destruction, so long as it came after he got to the top.

It was but a few steps away. His chest tightened more, his breathing grew shorter still. The voice continued to speak, he continued to listen. If he listened closely perhaps he could keep destruction at bay. Just ahead lay the final climb. He paused to gather strength.

For years this had been a place where he could come. Each year, even this year, he looked forward to coming. But next year? People who had made the place what it was (had been here for years, some of them) were leaving. Some died, some retired, others took jobs elsewhere. He could not be sure how long those who remained would stay. Vonnie, for example: she was not young. Next year she might not be here. Luann: she was not longtime. She might not be here either. And Kate was enceinte. She planned to stay at home, look after her baby. The old man did not begrudge her. He wished his mother had been so caring. But he would miss her smile, her warm greeting each morning. The faces he'd see would be new. He would be another guest, another face. If they smiled at him it was because they were told to. It would no longer be a place where he could come.

He looked up. The voice spoke, told him to complete what he had begun. All that remained was that kettlelike mass of rock. It was time to take it on.

●

Even when he was younger and fitter the final part was hard: a hundred yards, perhaps less. He sweated every inch. But the chance to look out on those mountains carried him to the top each time. He hoped it would carry him now: a triumph of the will over a body that had no business on this mountain.

He could see the summit. Sweat drenched his shirt, ran down his face so hard it blinded him. His body told him to quit, the voice told him to go on. He shut out pain, summoned gasps of breath.

He got there literally on hands and knees. The will had triumphed. He struggled onto his feet and, leaning on his stick, eyes salty from sweat, looked out on those neverending ranges. Pain rose in his belly, spread to his chest: the worst he had known. But his eyes remained fixed on those mountains.

●

Hikers found his body. They formed a team, carried it down mountain. One of them went to the front desk. Kate was working. She broke down in tears. She passed the news to Vonnie and Luann. They wept also. He was a sweet old man and they loved him. And now he was gone.

The hiker had more to say. When he and his comrades found the body they noticed something odd. Although he was dead a smile spanned the width of his face.

Ambi Bambi

First her sister phoned but got no answer. So she came over. She screamed, called 911. Within minutes an EMS team arrived. They notified the police. The cops checked out the body, the bottle of pills in her hand, the empty bottle of vodka. Then one of them stated the obvious: she drank too much booze, swallowed too many pills. A suicide: end of story.

But not so fast. This isn't over. I'm still interested.

Her name was Amber and she danced at a strip joint out by the interchange. We lived in the same building. She always gave a little smile, said "Hi." I said "Hi" back. That was all. But enough to say I knew her.

She'd been here a year, give or take. I knew little about her. Somebody told me she was girl of the month in a men's magazine years ago. If so I missed the issue.

So why'd she live here? Same reason I do: the rent's cheap. The neighbors are best described as sketchy. I'm never surprised when a cop car pulls into the parking lot, siren wailing, red light flashing. All I wonder is what came down this time. But I stay, and why? My wife took me to the cleaners when we divorced.

Can't say I blame her. I shouldn't have been messing with that babe in the business office at the newspaper where I was a reporter. We managed to keep our affair quiet until she got the guilties and told her husband. He stormed into the newsroom threatening to beat the crap out of me. I got canned on the spot. My inamorata got the axe too. I don't know what became of her. Never bothered to find out. After that my name was toxic. That's why I live from payday to payday (and most months not even that), working at an end of the road newspaper in an end of the road town in an end of the road part of the country.

Now, back to Amber. Or Ambi Bambi, as she was known professionally. She was in her thirties, slightly over medium height with platinum hair. Her face was hard though her eyes, light blue, were pretty. She had breasts so large they didn't seem real, but her stomach was flat as a board, all hers. Certainly I could see her gyrating on men's laps for a living. I bet they tipped well.

I feel for lapdancers. It's shitty work. How'd you like to strut your stuff with nothing on, roomful of horny guys shouting obscenities? Don't think you would.

And it can be dangerous. Years ago I covered a story about gunmen bursting into a massage parlor, lining the women against a wall and shooting them dead. Then torching the trailer the parlor was in. A mob hit, pure and simple.

I knew the son of one of those women: high school kid who ushered at the movieplex in the mall. Nice boy, always polite. That hit likely left him an orphan. (So, you ask, what about his dad? Gimme a break. That man was long out of that boy's life and I'll bet a steak dinner on that.)

You probably call that woman a whore. But what would you do if you had no marketable skills and a son to rear? Would you let him starve? Hell no. You'd take any job, even a lowlife one, to make sure he got fed.

Yes Ambi Bambi was a lapdancer with bottle blond hair and a boob job. But she always had that smile. That's why I'm sorry she'd dead. Sorry too something in her life made her swallow those pills.

I want to know what that something was.

●

News of her death is confined to a paragraph on an inside page. It gives bare facts, no more: dead in her apartment of an apparent overdose of prescription meds, no sign of foulplay: the end of a life told in two sentences.

I wish she hadn't killed herself on my day off. You see, I'm the police reporter. If I'd been working I would have done more than jot down a few facts. I would have asked questions. Gotten answers.

Sketchy though it is, the report provides information. Such as her name: Amber Lee Sweeten. And her age: thirtysix. But no mention of the magazine spread. Maybe that's hearsay. I want to know for sure.

One place to go is the internet. I'd rather not. It's wrecked the newspaper business, put too many of my fellow scribes out of work. But I go anyway. When you want information badly enough you're not picky about where you get it.

I type in the magazine's name and the word centerfold, hit the search key. And bingo: files flow like chips from a slot machine. I open one listing centerfolds by the year, scroll until I find the year in which Miss October was Amber Leeds. It's been sixteen years, but there's no doubt. Her breasts were smaller, round and firm; her hair a light brown: a nice girl with her life ahead of not behind her. Makes me wonder how she ended up lapdancing for losers in a city that began its losing streak years before she was born. When did her luck turn bad? And why?

●

I knock on the door to the managing editor's office. From within a husky voice bids me enter. I do.

She's a short and buxom, spiky black hair, huge tortoise shell glasses, pinstriped suit, skirt showing off legs that aren't bad. Her name is Samantha Whitten, but she goes by Sam, hates being called Sammy. I call her Sammy.

"Well," she says, peering through her glasses. Her eyes blend brown and green. "What is it now?"

"This morning's report about the suicide at the Sunset Apartments."

She tries to remember. Police news is not a priority. Soon after arriving she relegated it to single paragraph items in agate type far back in the paper.

"Sefton—" (the kid who works police on my day off and yes Sefton is his first name) "—missed the whole point of the story."

Without saying a word she picks up today's paper, leafs through until she reaches the page containing the police report. She scans it quickly.

"I think he covered it well." Figures: Sefton is a pet. I'm not. She's even tried to fire me. The Newspaper Guild saved my ass, bless them.

"The hell he did. There're more holes in it than a package of Swiss cheese."

"Well—" She drags out the word. "I don't see any."

I want to tell her she doesn't know shit from Shinola about police news. But my paycheck is important to me. "There's nothing about her being a centerfold in a men's magazine."

"I didn't know that."

"That's because it wasn't in the report. But she was, sixteen years ago. She was Miss October. She was also a movie actress." It's true. Her name appears at the bottom of cast lists as Hooker or Girl in Bikini #2: not the stuff of which Oscar nominations are made. "There should've been something about that."

After a space during which neither of us speaks she asks, "Is that all?"

"There's nothing about her being a dancer at the Turnpike Lounge."

"I'm not familiar with that establishment."

"It's a strip club. Been around a long time. Popular joint, particularly during happy hour. But I guess it's not exactly your type of place."

"No. It's not."

"She did lapdances there. Sammy, she used to be somebody. Then she became nobody. Now she's dead. That's a story."

"You're right. It is a story. But not one that appeals to me."

I want to scream "Bullshit" but all I say is "Why?"

Her eyes almost disappear behind those enormous glasses.

"A woman who would pose for one of those magazines and then work at a place like that? No. Hers is not a story that I wish to share with our readers."

"Look at it this way. She was sexually exploited, forced to demean herself. And it drove her to take her life. Doesn't that tug at your heartstrings?"

"It does not." Her lips become a line of red lipstick thin as paper. "There will be no story and that's that. So stop arguing with me."

I shrug. "Okay, Sammy. You're the boss."

She doesn't answer. I get up, head for the door.

"One moment please," she says. I turn around. "Maintenance informs me that they've found cigarette butts on the ground outside the rear exit. We allow members of our staff who persist in destroying their lungs to smoke there. But unless you stop throwing your butts on the ground we have no choice but to revoke the privilege." She doesn't ask if I'm one of the offenders. She knows. "Do I make myself clear?"

"Yeah." No "Yes ma'am," not even "Yes," just "Yeah." And I'm gone.

●

"Ya should of taken the buyout." Tommy gulps down whiskey. He's my buddy, used to work at the paper. We're drinking boilermakers in a saloon that's survived every hard time this town has seen. "So why didn't ya?"

"They didn't offer me enough."

"That's nuts."

"Maybe it is, but I didn't do it."

"Next time they won't be offerin t' buy ya out, they'll be handin ya a pinkslip. Ya should of done what I did—take the buyout."

Tommy Radovic was wire editor for more years than Sammy Whitten has been alive. When he finished school he didn't join his dad at the steel mill. He got a job at the paper, as a copyboy. It seemed a better bet. And it has been. The steel mills are closed. The paper is still publishing—for now.

"I'll take my chances."

"Ya should of taken 'em up."

"The money wasn't there."

"Bullshit. It was a good offer. Look at me. I'm not hurtin."

"But you're not paying alimony."

"That I'm not. Still married to the girl I was seein in high school. Been married fortyfive years, four kids, nine grandkids. But seriously, ya should of taken the money. Then ya wouldn't hafta put up with that snotty bitch."

"You have a point."

"Damn right I do. She's one reason I grabbed the offer. Didn't wanta listen to her anymore." He downs another shot, chases it with a long swallow of beer. "Remember when she just got here, time she wanted sushi n couldn't get any?"

I remember. You couldn't shut her up.

"Way she went on you'd of thought somebody'd raped her. Sushi, my ass. Where the hell'd she think she was gonna get sushi in this town?"

"Beats me." The closest thing to gourmet fare in these parts is the steamship round on the Sunday buffet at the Holiday Inn. And half the time you can't get it rare. "She's also never heard of the Turnpike Lounge."

"Yer shittin me."

"I am not."

"Jesus Mary n Joseph, everybody knows that place. It's a landmark."

"Want to know something, Tommy? The newspaper business is going to the dogs."

19

"That's an understatement."

"It's not just the internet, the layoffs, all that stuff. It's the people in charge. They all went to J school. They have that mindset. Back when I started you didn't need J school. You didn't even need a degree. I didn't have one."

"I thought ya had college."

"I dropped out, end of my sophomore year, and joined the army. When I got out I went to work at a paper in Pennsylvania. It even helped, not having a degree."

"Yeah? How's that?"

"Guy who hired me—oldtimer who worked his way to managing editor—he told me if I had a degree they'd have to pay me more. That's how I got the job. I didn't finish college and they could hire me cheaper. But now? Instead of a crusty pro who paid his dues there's Sammy Whitten with her big glasses and halfbaked ideas. I just hope I can hang on till I peg out—which may not be too far off."

"Aw c'mon—"

"It's true. I smoke a pack a day, I'm fifty pounds overweight, I eat the wrong food, don't get enough sleep, my only exercise is walking from my apartment to the car, and sometimes I have trouble peeing. So maybe the big one'll get me before the You Know What hits the Westinghouse."

"Jeez yer an optimist. Now, changin the subject, the girl ya told me bout, the one that killed herself—ya still doin a story on her?"

I nod.

"Didn't Sammy tell ya t' lay off?"

"She did. But I'm doing it anyway."

"The paper won't print it."

"But someplace else might. I know a guy at the National Enquirer."

"Why're ya so interested in her?"

"I knew her. I'd see her round the building. We'd say 'Hi,' she'd smile. Yeah. She always had that smile for me."

"Anything else?"

"I'd like to know why she went from centerfold to dancing at the Turnpike."

"How ya gonna find out? Ya can't talk t' her. She's dead."

"People knew her. I can talk to them. Hell I'm not doing her life story. All I want to know is what started her down that slippery slope."

"N that's it?"

"Yep."

"Ya sure?"

"Yes Tommy. I'm sure."

"Sometimes ya get mixed up in the stories ya cover. So there's nothin else?"

"Not a thing, Tommy. Not a thing."

He says nothing more. Maybe he knows I won't tell the truth.

●

Detective Sergeant Tosco shakes his head. "She didn't leave a note. Most a them do. But not this time."

If he had something he'd tell me. He always does. If, say, a drug bust goes down he lets me know and I keep mum until after it happens. He knows I will. That's the thing with the gendarmes. They have to trust you. Otherwise you get silence. They trust me, so they tell me what they have.

But this time Sergeant Tosco hasn't got a thing.

"You're kidding me," I tell him.

He shakes his head. "Nope. She's clean as a whistle."

"That's unusual."

"Yeah. But she worked at the Turnpike. Ya know how it is there."

I do. Never a bust, not one disturbance on file: a clean operation—unless they're paying off the cops. That's always a possibility.

"Not even a DUI or a parking ticket?"

"Lemme see." He goes to a computer, types in her name. "Yeah. Bout six months ago. Pulled over for speedin, drivin erratic. They gave her a Breathalyzer test but it came up borderline. They let her go, cited her for speedin."

"That's all you've got?"

"Yeah. That's it. Say, why the interest in this girl?"

"She always smiled at me."

Sergeant Tosco laughs. "Well, okay. Good luck, pal."

"Thanks, Lou."

●

I know the Turnpike's manager. Roy Fitzer. He's a character: big and beefy, still wears leisure suits and loud polyester shirts, gold pendants resting on a hairy chest. He's a blast from the Seventies, like lava lamps and the Bee Gees. But he doesn't care. He's always worn leisure suits, must have a dozen in his closet.

The joint is nearly deserted. On stage a dancer named Destiny hugs the pole like she's making love. I scan the room, dark as night though it's one in the afternoon, and see Roy at a corner table. I walk over.

He leans back in his chair, eyes me warily. "What can I do fer ya?" he says. We've never had trouble, but the sight of me doesn't send a thrill up his leg.

"I want to talk to you about a woman who used to work here."

"Yeah? Which one?"

"Amber Sweeten."

A scowl creases his blocky face. "She killed herself. So what's it t' ya?"

"I knew her."

"So'd half the guys in town. What makes ya so special?"

"We lived in the same building. We'd see each other several times a week."

"So now ya wanta do a story. What kind a story?"

"Nothin sensational, if that's what's bugging you. She seemed like a nice person, always had a smile for me. I want to find out why she did it. That's all."

The scowl goes away. "Okay. Siddown."

I sit across from him. I want to look him in the eye.

"She was my best dancer. My customers was crazy bout her."

"Did she do lapdances?"

The scowl is back. "Hey. I thought ya wasn't doin a job on me."

"I'm not. Trust me."

"Okay. Y've never given me heartburn. Lemme just say I run a clean establishment. Been here for years n never had no trouble. Never."

"I know that. But what about your girls?"

"My girls do lapdances, nothin more. Get what I'm sayin?"

I do.

"If any a my girls're doin tricks on my time they're gone. They can't even make dates with the customers. What they do on their time's their concern. But here at the club I don't allow no monkeybus'ness."

"I get your point, Roy."

"Good. Now what ya wanta know bout Amber?"

"How long did she work here?"

"Year, maybe. Could of been longer. She moved here from California."

"Did she say why?"

"Nah. Just showed up one day askin for a job. Lucky for her I had one."

"Did you ever have trouble with her?"

Again, the scowl. "Didn't I just tell ya? She was my best dancer."

"The police stopped her about six months ago. They thought she might have been drinking."

"Yeah. She did have that problem."

"Did it affect her work?"

"One day she called in, said she wasn't feelin good. I knew she wasn't sick, but I let it slide. I should of said somethin. Wish I had."

"But other than that you had no trouble."

"Nope. She didn't miss another day till—"

He heaves a sigh. I don't ask him to finish. Even tough guys have a heart.

"Real nice kid," he says at last. "I miss the hell out a her."

I miss her too, miss her smiles. But I have a job to do. "Were there men?"

"I told ya, I run a clean bus'ness."

"I'm talking about boyfriends. Did she have any?"

"Yeah. She mentioned a guy, once. But that ended before she started here."

"Is that why she left California?"

"Maybe. She never did say why she left."

"Did men come by to see her?"

"Sure they did. She was my most popular dancer."

"Not the customers. Did anyone stop by just to talk?"

"Yeah. There was one. She went over to his table after her act was over. They talked a while, then he got up n left."

"Was he the only one?"

"Yeah. But next day she didn't come in, didn't call in sick. Didn't put the two together, don't know why. Usually I'm good at spottin trouble. God I wish I'd of been that time. Real good girl, Ambi Bambi. Just the best. What a waste."

"Thanks. You've been a help."

"Glad to be a service." He shakes his head. "What a waste. What a sad frickin waste."

●

Her sister is as wary as Roy Fitzer but for another reason.

"She's dead," she says through a crack in the door. "Can't you let it go?"

"This is different."

She asks how.

"We lived in the same building. We'd see each other." The wary look recedes. "She was a nice person. Every time she saw me she smiled. Every time."

Now a smile, faint but visible. "That was Amber. Okay. C'm in."

She shows me into the livingroom. Her husband is working on the loading dock at Kroger, the kids are at school. She invites me to sit on the sofa.

"What ya wanta know bout my sister?" she says after I'm seated.

"What made her do what she did?"

"It's not what ya think. Yeah she was in that magazine. N yeah she danced at that club. But she wasn't that kind a person. Not that kind at all."

She pauses, takes a deep breath. She looks nothing like Ambi Bambi: chunky, flat face, mousy hair.

"She was the sweetest human bein. Always kind, wasn't a thing she wouldn't do for ya. But—" Again she pauses. "She was too pretty for her own good. Always was. N she never did attract the right kind a man."

They never do, those sweet pretty ones. Ambi Bambi's story takes a turn I should have seen from the start.

"She had this guy. Met him in high school, kept datin him after they graduated. Nicelookin guy, snappy dresser. But he had—oh what should I say?—yeah he had some character flaws, some big ones."

I don't ask which ones. She goes on:

"He started foolin with another girl n Amber broke up with him. It hurt her, bigtime. I think that's why she posed for those pictures, t' get back at him. He married this new girl n she couldn't deal with it. Even with her new life out there in Los Angeles, modelin n bein in the movies: none a that helped. She was still carryin the torch. N she didn't care for the guys she met out there. They seen her pictures in the magazine n well— She didn't want 'em. She wanted Mr Right. But she never could find him. So she left LA, started dancin. She was good at it n the money was good too. Then maybe a year n a half back he showed up out a the blue, said him n his wife'd split n he'd like t' see her again. N she said yes. It was stupid but she did it anyways. N she got hurt. That's when she moved here. I'm all the fam'ly she's got n she wanted t' be near me. At first it was good. She'd come n see me, I'd go n see her. We'd have lunch, maybe go to the mall, do some shoppin. Then she stopped comin by, began drinkin again. She'd started drinkin out in LA. She had a big problem, drinkin. Kept sayin she was gonna stop, join AA, but she never did. Then one day he came by the club. Told her he was back with his wife n this time it was for good. He wanted t' tell her in person, no emails or nothin. That was good a him, bad for her. And— Well, I guess ya know the rest." She brushes away a tear. "He broke her heart so many times she couldn't take it no more. That's what she said in her note."

"The police said there wasn't any note."

"That's cause I didn't give it to 'em."

"You broke the law."

"I did?"

"Yes. You withheld evidence in an investigation."

"So what if I did? It's none a their bus'ness, what was in that note."

"What did you do with it?"

"I read it n tore it up n flushed it down the toilet."

"Can you tell me what was in it?"

She shakes her head as hard as she can. "It was addressed t' me. N I'm not tellin anyone what's in it—not you, not the cops, not even my husband. What she wrote's between me n her n that's how it's gonna stay."

"Okay."

"Thanks. I 'preciate that."

"For what it's worth I truly am sorry. She was a nice person. I mean that."

She looks sat me. Her eyes are red from crying.

"Ya b'lieve in angels, sir?" she says.

Now I'm the one shaking my head.

"Well, I do. I b'lieve each n every one of us has our own special angel that's watchin over us, makin sure we're okay. N I b'lieve Amber is one a those angels, watchin over both me n you."

I don't answer. I don't know how I can.

"I'm sorry to have taken up your time."

She manages a smile. "Don't worry bout it. It—it gave me a chance t' talk bout Amber. She wasn't what people thought she was."

"No. She wasn't." I prepare to leave.

"Ya gonna write anything bout this for the paper?"

I shake my head one last time. Ambi Bambi's story is over. But mine goes on. I wonder when it will end.

Ballad of a Simple Man

Gary Beeler was a simple man, proud of the label. He didn't want to be president of the United States or a hall of famer, an astronaut or a movie star. All he wanted was to be happy and content.

He put roofing on houses and was good at it. That meant he always had work. He would never be rich. But he made enough money to provide for his family and make payments on the prefab house they lived in, the bedroom and livingroom suites, and the Ford Focus sedan (but not the pickup truck: that was paid for), with a little put aside for a rainy day. Anything more was sheer luck.

He was happy in his life. Jamie was an angel. He said that time and again. And it was the truth. Jamie was all the woman he wanted, the only women he'd ever wanted. He never gave other women a second look.

They'd dated through high school, were married on the Saturday after commencement. Ten months later she gave birth to a baby girl.

"Let's call her Angel," he said.

She asked why.

"Cause yer an angel n she's gonna grow up to be an angel just like you."

So the baby got her name: Angel Marie Beeler.

His life was complete. He had a family: not of birth but of his making.

Jamie was a born mother and from within himself he found the ability to be a father. He doted on the baby, dandling her on his knee and singing to her. She couldn't understand a word but enjoyed his singing. He knew from her smile. It was a pretty smile that made him want to do things that brought it out often.

He took turns getting up in the middle of the night to change her diaper, hold her against his shoulder, pat her gently so she'd stop crying, get her back to sleep: something Dad never did. Not once did he complain, even when tired from work and craving unbroken sleep.

Yes Gary Beeler had what he called a good life: a happy life, a contented life. A life he hoped he could live for the rest of his days.

Then one Friday afternoon as he was getting off from work Ron Eshelman his foreman called him over to say the boss wanted to see him.

Gary Beeler went right away.

Earl First was not a bad man. Nor was he a mean man. He was a man who owned a business and if he was going to remain in business he had to make money. And right now not enough money was being made.

All this he explained to Gary Beeler who listened but asked no questions. Then he said, "I'm gonna hafta let ya go."

Gary Beeler wanted to say something but couldn't. He was too stunned.

"It's not a decision I take pleasure in," Earl First said. "Surely not. But the economy's in the tank n it looks like it's gonna stay there a while, so—Well, Gary, truth is I got no choice."

At last Gary Beeler opened his mouth: "But why me?"

Earl First cleared his throat. "Like I said I got no choice."

"But I've always showed up on time, always done my day's work, work overtime every time I'm asked n I almost never call in sick. So why's it me?"

"It's the rules."

Now Gary Beeler understood: "Last hired, first fired."

"Exactly. Yer a good man, Gary, best I got. But the contract says—"

"I know what it says."

Indeed he did. Workers were furloughed on the basis of seniority. The union had insisted on that. And if you worked certain jobs in the commonwealth of Pennsylvania, you had to join the union, follow its rules.

Gary Beeler had done that. And had just got the worst screwing of his life.

Earl First attempted a smile. "I'm gonna miss ya. We're all gonna miss ya. But rules're rules."

"I'm sorry too, Mr First. I like workin for ya n I don't know where I'm gonna find a job like this."

"Y'll find one. May take a while, but one'll turn up, I guarantee it."

"Maybe yer right." But, Gary Beeler thought, not likely.

"It's nothin personal," Earl First said. "Hope y' unnerstand."

"Yeah. I unnerstand," But Gary Beeler meant not a word.

"Ya can pick up yer pay from Gloria in accounting. I told her to get it ready for ya. I also told her to put in a little extra: ya know, a sign a my appreciation."

"Thanks." Gary Beeler didn't mean that either.

"Good luck," Earl First said and rose, held out his hand. Gary Beeler shook it. "Yeah. I'm gonna need it."

This time he meant every word.

After picking up his pay (which he tucked into his shirt pocket) he drove to the Town Talk Tavern, his usual stop after work.

"Hey Freddie, gimme a shot," he shouted to the bartender.

"Sure, Gary. But aint it usually a beer?"

"I'm havin one. But I want a shot too. N I'm drinkin it over there."

He pointed to a booth at the rear of the dimly lighted room.

"Yer just full a surprises today," Freddie said.

"What ya mean?"

"First the shot n now ya wanta sit back there."

"What's so strange bout that?"

"Y' always like t' sit here at the bar."

"Maybe I want a little privacy."

"Sure, Gary. Yer the boss." Freddie paused. "Rough day?"

"Yeah. Real rough."

"Wanta talk bout it?"

"Nah."

Gary Beeler walked to the booth and sat down. Freddie brought a shot glass of whiskey and a mug of beer, set them on the table. Gary Beeler drank the whiskey in one shot and then half of the beer.

"Bring me another," he said. Freddie did.

He nursed this one. And did some thinking. Since marrying Jamie he had kept the family sheltered and fed, paid the bills. Now he would not have money for that. Yes there was unemployment, but that didn't last forever.

Then what? Would he have a job by the time it ran out? Would it pay like the old one did? Could he still make the payments on the house, the car, the furniture, all the stuff he and Jamie had bought on time? Or would they lose it all? He had no answers. When he got up this morning he thought he knew his future. Now he was sure of nothing.

One thing he did know: Jamie must be told. She would not like hearing what he had to tell. And he would not like telling it.

He finished the shot, slurped the last of the beer. It was time to go home, break the news. Or face the music: that seemed more like it. He paid his tab and walked out the door and into the pickup, put the key in the ignition switch.

"Yer late," Jamie said as he stumbled through the door.

"Yeah. I know."

"N ya been drinkin whiskey."

"A little."

"More'n a little, I'd say. I can smell it from where I'm standin."

"Okay. I had two shots."

"Y' usually have beer."

"This time I had whiskey too."

"We went ahead n ate, me n Angel. I kept some for ya. It's in the oven."

She brought him a plate of meatloaf and mashed potatoes and peas. He began eating. The food was good. It always was: one of her many gifts.

"Okay," she said. "What happened?"

He looked at her but did not answer. A piece of meatloaf was impaled on the fork suspended between his plate and his mouth.

"Somethin happened. N it wasn't good. I can tell by the look in yer eyes."

He swallowed the meatloaf.

"I lost my job."

It was her turn to be silent. Then: "Did I hear ya right?"

"Ya did."

She placed her hands on her stomach. Her face looked as if she'd turned ill.

"Oh my God," she said. "It can't be true—"

"Well, it is. I got laid off."

"Why? Why you?"

He explained.

"They let ya go cause ya was the low man?" she said after he was finished.

He nodded sadly

"So what're we gonna do?"

"Beats me."

"We gotta do somethin."

"Yeah."

"But what?"

"I don't know."

"What ya mean ya don't know? Ya gotta know somethin."

"Look, baby. Mr First just told me. I haven't had time t' figure it out."

"There's got t' be another job out there."

"Maybe."

"Just maybe?"

"I gotta know where it is before I can find it."

"What's that mean?"

"Means times're bad. Means not many houses're bein sold. Means not many're bein built. Means people aint hirin. They're firin instead."

"So y' aint gonna find another job?"

"I didn't say that. I said it aint gonna be easy."

"So what d' we do in the meantime?"

"I'll go on unemployment."

"Oh my God."

"Least the bills get paid, some a them anyway. It could be worse."

"Oh Gary, why'd this hafta happen?"

"I told you—I was the last one hired. Means I was the first t' get fired."

"It don't seem fair."

"No. It don't. But it's how it's done."

"Ya gonna look for another job?"

"First thing tomorrow mornin."

She smiled. "That's my man."

In bed she cuddled, began kissing.

"Stop that," he said.

"Why?"

"Aint in the mood."

"Y' always been in the mood before."

"Well, I aint in it now."

"Is it the job?"

"Yeah."

"Maybe I can take yer mind off of it. So let's do it. It's worked before."

But it didn't. His heart was not in it and that spoiled it for both of them. After they finished (sooner than usual) they rolled over, backsides facing one another. She fell asleep; he remained awake a while longer.

●

That was one year ago. Gary Beeler is still out of work. At first he answered every want ad, followed up every lead. But none led to a job. He has given up trying. When someone makes a suggestion he throws up his hands.

"What's the use?" he says. "All they're gonna say is no."

"How ya know they will?"

"I just know."

"But ya haven't tried."

"I know what they're gonna say, what they always say—no. That's all I been hearin for a year now."

But something must happen, soon. Next month his jobless benefits run out. He hopes for a miracle. But miracles don't happen to people like him.

Things haven't changed, everything has changed. He and Jamie now live apart. They remain married, have no plans to divorce.

The longer he was out of work the harder it got for them to stay together. Gainful employment continued to elude him, but she found work: not steady, but it brought in money. She cleaned houses, helped at a daycare center: worked here a little, there a little, most of the time stayed busy.

But he had no such luck. Drinking beer and watching TV, yelling at Angel to be quiet, ordering her to her room if she wasn't: that was all he had to do.

Finally Jamie moved out.

"I can't take it no more," she said. "I mean it. I can't go on like this."

"What ya gonna do?"

"Move back in with Mom. N take Angel with me."

"So yer leavin—"

She nodded.

"It aint gonna work, livin with Hazel. Two a y'll be at it inside of a day."

"That's for me t' find out." Silence, then: "Ya know I love ya, honey. But I can't live with ya. Right now I can't."

"Hope this aint for good."

"I hope it aint either." She tried to smile. It didn't work. "Hey sweetie. I don't like this either."

"Then why the hell ya doin it?"

"Cause I gotta. I can't put up with this any longer."

"That's what ya said."

"Please, Gary. Try n unnerstand."

"I can't."

"I was afraid a that."

She was gone and so was Angel. He was alone with his beer and his TV and his regrets and above all his failure to land a job after all these months.

After a while (and not a long while at that) he got tired of this. He wanted to see Jamie again, wanted to see Angel again. He wanted them to come home.

So he called Jamie, asked when she was coming back. She said she wasn't.

He asked if that was for now or for all time.

She said she couldn't say.

He said he was tired of living in the house without her or Angel there.

She said that was too bad, but she couldn't live with him, at least not now.

He said he understood. But he didn't understand, probably never would.

She said she was glad he did, but he figured she knew he was lying.

Then, an idea: "What say I move out n you n Angel come back here n live?"

"Where ya gonna stay?"

"With my brother. Beats bein alone. And there'd be people in the house."

She said she liked the idea. Then she said yes.

He had no money, but she had some coming in from jobs she did. So he asked if she'd mind making the payments on the house and the furniture and the Ford Focus which she was driving. She said she didn't mind.

She and Angel moved back into the house and he moved in with his brother Nelson. He hoped the day would come when he could return to the house and he and Jamie and Angel would be a family again.

He hoped it would come sooner, not later.

But now it looks like it will come later.

He's still at Nelson's place. It's in the next town, about eight miles away: an apartment in an old house in a street of old houses, most of which have also been carved into apartments. Paint flakes off woodwork, weeds and grass sprout in narrow lawns. But it's a place where he can stay.

Nelson, who is divorced, charges no rent. That is something Gary Beeler can afford.

And maybe his luck will change. This town is the county seat, larger by three thousand people. More people mean more things going on and (if he's lucky) a job he can do, someone who will let him do it. If that happens maybe Jamie will take him back.

But maybe doesn't get him a job. Maybe doesn't get Jamie back. Maybe just leaves him where he is and that's not good enough.

His life is like the one back at the house: alone all day while Nelson is at the toothbrush plant where he's a supervisor. It's hard to amuse yourself when all you can afford is to sit around.

He goes for a walk, heads downtown. The main street is lined with brick buildings of two or three stories. The ground floors are storefronts but few businesses occupy them. Most wear a look of better days gone by. Other storefronts are empty, windows so begrimed you can't see through them.

He has seen enough, returns to the apartment. Plops onto the sofa, presses the remote. A soap opera emerges. The story is as sad as the life he lives. But he watches anyway. One of the actresses reminds him of Jamie. Her figure is trim while Jamie's is not. But the eyes, the smile are the same. Memories are stirred, the body aches. He can watch no longer. The screen goes dark.

The apartment contains no books. Even if it did he would not pick up one. He'd read his last book in high school. Nor is there a newspaper. Again no loss: he doesn't follow the news. If he had he might have anticipated losing his job. There is a computer. But delights of the internet, even of games, do not appeal.

He sits, alone, in a small room with only sofa and lamp, a table with the TV set on it. The windows have no curtains, so he can look outside if he wishes. He does not wish. There is nothing out there he hasn't seen before. All he can do is think. But he doesn't want to. All that is left is to exist. And existing is not enough.

He goes into the kitchen, removes two slices of bread from the wrapper, a slice of bologna from the refrigerator, combines them in a sandwich and eats it. Then reaches back into the fridge, retrieves a can of beer. Snaps it open, drinks its contents. Nourished, he returns to the livingroom and lies down on the sofa.

A door slams shut, rousing him. Slowly his eyes open to see Nelson standing in the middle of the room. Nelson doesn't get off until four, so he must have slept all afternoon. But no, the clock reads two fifteen.

"Hey there, bud," Nelson says.

Gary Beeler lets out a sleepy grunt.

"Got some news."

"Yeah? What?"

"There's a job for ya. I tried t' call but ya didn't pick up."

"Sorry."

"No problem. Anyway I told the boss I knew somebody n I wanted t' tell him n he said okay. So y' interested, bud?"

Though foggy from sleep Gary Beeler grasps the importance of the moment.

"Damn right. What do I gotta do?"

"Get yer ass over there n put in for it, that's what. N when ya see the boss tell him I sent ya. He'll know what yer talkin bout."

Gary Beeler rises, stretches his stocky body.

"Better put on a fresh shirt," Nelson says. "One ya got on's all wrinkled."

Gary Beeler roots rummages through his clothes, pulls out a shirt. Takes off the wrinkled shirt, puts on the clean one. Nelson wishes him luck, but he's already out the door.

At the toothbrush plant he asks to see the boss.

"Is he expecting you?" the receptionist asks.

"I'm the guy Nelson Beeler told him bout."

She shows him into the boss's office. Five minutes later he comes out with a job. The pay is not half of what he took in as a roofer, the benefits are minimal. But it's honest work he may be doing for a while. The construction business is hurting, but folks still buy toothbrushes.

Yes it's a job and that's more than he's had for twelve hard months.

Celebration is in order. He chooses the Castaway Lounge. It's a bit of the South Seas in Pennsylvania: plenty of bamboo and fake palm trees that can't conceal the fact it's another tavern favored by working stiffs like him. He takes a seat at the bar.

"What ya got on tap?" he asks the bartender.

"Miller n Bud."

"Gimme a Miller."

He nurses the beer, lets it roll against his palate before swallowing. Save for him and the bartender the place is empty. He says nothing, works his beer slowly. Mark the moment: his moment. The bartender understands. He keeps his distance until Gary Beeler finishes his beer, asks for another.

The bartender sets it down. This time he doesn't take it so slowly. No longer need he bury his head in shame. No longer must he pity himself. He has rejoined the world. And he is happy about that.

As he drinks an idea forms.

Now he can go home. Talk to Jamie, work things out. Maybe now he has a job life can return to what it was.

It's worth a try.

He pays the bartender, stuffs a dollar bill in the tip jar. As he rises from his stool he has trouble steadying himself.

"Y' all right, mister?" the bartender asks.

"Never been better."

"Okay. Take care."

"Will do."

And he should take care. The road is a twisting affair riddled with potholes neither state nor county has funds to fix. For part of the way it passes through thick forest teeming with game.

But Gary Beeler doesn't think of this as he speeds as fast as (and sometimes faster than) the law allows. His thoughts are of Jamie, the news he has. Of becoming husband and father again. Of anything but the perils along the way.

He thinks nothing of them until he hears a thud, then tinkling of glass as the windshield shatters, and in one final second he sees a huge deer crashing on him.

A Game

First I ask how she got here. It's a barroom in an old mining town so deep in backcountry the rich and famous are just now learning it exists and it's the middle of the afternoon and she's tending bar and I'm her only customer.

"Followed a guy," she tells. "He moved on, I didn't."

I sip the beer she has poured for me. "Why didn't you?"

"Didn't feel like it."

Not much of an answer. I change tack.

"What's your name?"

"Karla. N it's spelled with a K not a C."

"Unusual spelling."

"Blame my parents. They named me." She smiles. It's a nice smile. "But I don't mind. It's different."

"So, Karla with a K, where are you from?"

"Lots a places."

"Such as?"

"Where do you want me to start?"

"I get the picture."

"Figured you would."

"I've lived in lots of places too."

"Yeah? Like where?"

"Where it's suited me to live."

"Funny answer."

"But true. When it no longer suits me to live somewhere I pick up and move to a place where it does."

"N when that place no longer suits you—"

"I find some other place."

"Neat. Wish I could do that."

"Can't you?"

"Not always. But there of been times when I could, like it was my choice."

"Was it your choice to stay when that guy left?"

She has blue eyes that turn to ice when she wants them to. They do now.

"Yeah." And, after a space, "It was."

I say nothing. The glare vanishes. She says, "Albert Duggan's place on the edge a town, one he rents out for the summer. You're staying there, right?"

This is my first venture into town, yet she knows who I am. I ask how.

"This's a very small place. Somebody new comes in, words gets around. N I want it to get to me first."

I get her. This is where people come to drink socially. She makes their drinks. So she wants to know who they are.

I finish my beer. She asks if I want another. I say no, reach for my wallet.

"Hey. You don't hafta pay." She lets out a laugh I wish I heard more often.

"I don't?"

"Nah. It's on me. You made my afternoon."

"I did?"

"Yeah. Most a the time it's just me n my lonesome. You kept me company. So the beer's on me, okay?"

"Thanks. But can I leave a tip?"

"You don't hafta do that either."

"But what if I want to?"

She laughs again. "Can't stop you, can I?"

I leave a sawbuck on the bar.

"Wow. Some tip."

"Not where I come from."

"Most times all I get's like a dollar—if that." She sighs. "They got the money, people moving here these days. But they aren't very generous."

"I'm not generous either."

"But why me? Why now?"

"Because I enjoy your company, Karla with a K."

She says thanks. Says it with a smile. I get up, head for the door.

"See you tomorrow?" she says.

"Maybe."

"Same time?"

"Maybe."

"Be looking for you."

I say goodbye, nothing more.

●

The following afternoon I'm back.

"Hey," she says with a sly smile that goes well with the rest of her: blue eyes that turn to ice on command. Long black hair. A face that's faded but still catches the eye. She's had rough years—you can see them in that face, the snake tattooed around her left wrist—yet she remains desirable. Yes there's something about Karla with a K I find irresistible.

I say "Hey" back to her.

"I know why you moved here," she says and slides a beer across the bar.

"You do?"

"Yeah. You're writing a book."

I haven't told her, have told nobody, not even Alfred Duggan. All I told him was I needed the cabin. So I ask how she knows.

"You look like somebody that writes books," she says. "You know: thick glasses, horn rims. Thin hair combed over the scalp to make it look like you got more hair than you do. N I bet you wear tweed jackets n smoke a pipe."

She describes me to a T. But— "That doesn't make me a writer."

"Yes it does."

"All right. Have it your way."

"You're not the first one to do that, come here n write a book."

"I'm not?"

"Man came last year to write one, just like you. He even rented Alfred Duggan's cabin. Just like you."

"Did you meet him?"

"Nah. He holed up in the cabin, hardly ever came out."

"Did you see him?"

"Once. Saw him walk to the postoffice."

"Did he have hornrimmed glasses, comb his hair over his scalp?"

"Didn't get that good of a look."

"So how do you know he was a writer?"

"People said he was."

"How did they know? I'm sure he didn't tell them."

"They just knew."

"Just like you know I'm a writer—"

"Yeah. Just like that."

"What if he wasn't a writer? What if I'm not?"

"Then they were wrong. I'm wrong. But I don't think so."

"You don't?"

She shakes her head. "I think you're writing a book, but you don't want to tell me. That's cool. Don't tell me if you don't want to. But I know anyway: you're writing a book. That's what you're doing."

I'm good with that. Let her think I'm writing the Great American Novel. Let her think anything she wants. But only I know and I'm not saying.

It has become a game. She asks and I don't answer. Perhaps she doesn't expect me to. If I do the game will be over. There will be no more fun.

●

"Hey it's Writer Man," she shouts, laughing, as I arrive at what has become my usual time. She has even poured my usual beer. "Get any writing done?"

Laughing also: "That's for me to know and you to find out."

"So you did—"

"I didn't say that. I've never even said I'm writing a book."

"You don't hafta say it. I know."

"You're just guessing."

"Sometimes guessing's as good as knowing." She lets out a laugh so loud it could trigger a rockslide. "Hey. Am I in the book?"

"What book?"

"You know the one."

"All right, Karla with a K. Suppose I am writing a book—"

"Aha. So you really are writing one—"

"No. Just suppose I am. I'm talking, you know, hypothetically."

"I get you."

"Good. What if one of the characters is based on you? Would you mind?"

A pause. Then, "You wouldn't use my real name, would you?"

I shake my head.

"You mean that?"

"I wouldn't say it if I didn't."

"Thanks. I don't wanta see my name in a book—" (the foxy smile returns) "—even the one you say you're not writing."

"But you wouldn't mind, so long as I don't use your name—"

"God no. I'd be honored. Like me—a character in a book?"

"So, Karla with a K, if I do write a book—and I do mean if—you will be in it, but with a different name. Now—I have a question."

"Shoot."

"Would the character based on you really be you?"

"Course it'd be me. Who else would it be?"

"Good question. I know you're Karla with a K who thinks I'm writing a book. But that's all. I don't know anything else about you."

"Such as?"

"Where you're from and why you're here, miles from anywhere."

"Didn't I tell you? I came with a guy. He moved on, I stayed."

"But you didn't say why you stayed."

"I just did, that's why."

"There has to be more than that."

"Okay. I like it here. The money's not great, but I don't need much. N it gives me space. Yeah lots a space. Isn't that why you came here—to get space?"

She's right. I, like her, wanted space. But that's not what I got. Instead I got a very small place where people make it their business to know mine.

"Have you found that space?" I ask.

"Yeah. I do my own thing, nobody hassles me. Yeah, I got it. I got space."

"I'm glad you do. Sorry I can't say the same for myself."

"You mean all the questions I've been asking?"

"Questions I won't answer. But I'm not mad at you, Karla with a K. In fact I like you. I enjoy talking with you."

"So you don't mind when I ask you stuff?"

"Not one bit. You see, it's a game. You ask, I try not to answer."

"But how bout when I don't answer your questions?"

"It's part of the game."

She laughs. And then smiles. "I'm always glad to see you, Writer Man. You make my day."

And she makes mine. But I don't tell her. Better to let her guess.

●

Every afternoon I drop by, we talk. I don't answer her questions, she dodges mine. That's how we like it. As I said, it's a game.

Then one afternoon I stop by, usual time, and she's not there.

"She's off," the man behind the bar tells me. He's tall and blond, rugged looking. Must be Jody, her boss. "She wanted a couple days off n I let her have 'em. Can I get you something?"

I say no thanks.

"You must be the guy that come in every afternoon. Karla's told me bout you."

I say nothing, let him talk.

"She likes seeing you. It's slow here, afternoons. Real slow."

"Sure is." I don't want to tell this guy any more than I must.

"Sometimes I wonder why I open so early. There's no profit in it. But it gives her a job n Lord knows she needs it."

I want to ask why she needs the gig, he extends hours and pays her to work them. But I don't.

"You want a beer?" he says. "Karla says y' always have a beer."

"Not today." I turn toward the door.

"She'll be back Thursday," he shouts as I leave. I don't answer, think instead of Karla with a K. And wonder if he's the reason she decided to stay.

●

Finding her isn't hard. She lives in a cabin maybe a half mile outside town, up a narrow cañon through which a clear stream flows. It's pretty, wildflowers carpeting either side of the stream, aspens on mountainsides. I can't say what it's like in winter. By the time winter comes I'll be gone.

Karla with a K emerges wearing a bikini that leaves nothing to the imagination. A tattoo depicting a skull resting on a heart defaces much of her right upper thigh and hip. Her figure like her face is not what it once was, but she still has a fine pair of breasts that may or may not be real. I say they're not. But they still look good. She still looks good. Seeing her now triggers a serious case of lust.

"Hey Writer Man," she shouts in a way that lets me know she's happy to see me.

"You could have told me you'd be off." I laugh so as not to appear angry.

"Sorry. Should of said something. So how'd you find me? Jody tell you?"

"He didn't have to. I knew."

"You did? How?"

"Like you said, it's a very small place."

"Yeah. It is. Hey—" She walks over, gives a hug. It's real and it's tight, like a hug should be. Her almost naked body wrapped around me makes me lust more. I try not to let it show. "—Thanks for coming out."

"But your space? Isn't that why you took time off, to have space?"

"Yeah. But you're welcome to join me." She looks at me with those eyes, blue but not icy. "I mean it. So c'mon in. Got beer if you want it."

We step inside. She invites me to sit; I do. Then she reaches into the fridge, pulls out a can of beer. Pops it open, hands it to me. And sits across from me.

"Aren't you having a beer too?" I ask.

"Nah. Gonna smoke some weed."

She lights a joint, inhales, offers it to me. I shake my head.

"It's good shit. N don't worry, it's legal now."

"I know. But I'll pass anyway."

"Okay."

I look around. "This yours?"

"Nah. Belongs to Jody. He lets me stay here."

So that's it. She was done with the other man, hooked up with Jody instead.

"I know what you're thinking," she says. "You think me n Jody're having sex. Well, we did, after I got here. We even lived together for a while."

"Okay." Every word she says peels away the mystery. She becomes a woman of whom I know too much. She goes on: "We're friends now. Good friends. Tight. But the sex? That's done."

"I believe you."

"Just wanta make it clear."

She gets up, asks if I want another beer. I do. She gets it for me. But she doesn't sit down. She remains standing, looks me over.

"Know something, Writer Man?" she says. "I could go for you. Yeah I could go for you real bad."

I could go for her too. Her face, her body may be past their prime, but the sight of her in that bikini makes me want her in a big way.

I turn away, to a picture on a table by the chair on which she sat. It is of a small boy. I don't know his name. But I know who he is, why his picture is there. She hasn't said a word. She doesn't have to. I look again at the picture, then at her. Now I know for sure. Know also why I can't have her.

I chug my beer, rise to my feet. Tell her it's time to go. She doesn't want me to. I don't want to either. But part of me says I must. I listen.

She gives me another hug, lets it last a while. And then I'm gone.

The game is over.

●

I tell Alfred Duggan I'm leaving, pack up, load the car. I don't even stop by the bar to say goodbye.

●

I wish I had. Then she wouldn't wonder. Nor would I. Would not wonder what has become of her, whether she's got her life together, her son back with her, or whether she still drifts from town to town, man to man. It's been a couple of years, and I still wonder. And wish her well.

Now, about the book. Yes I had planned to write one but never did. When I got to the next town I couldn't get started. Maybe the book was never there.

But there is a story. It is not what I intended to write. But it's what got written. And this is it.

One final thing: Karla is not her real name. I made it up. I promised I wouldn't use her name, and one thing I have learned is when you give a woman your word it's best not to break it.

Heartland

"This story has been done so many times you're probably wondering why we're doing it again," my editor says after sitting me down in his office high above streets thronged with people who from this lofty perch appear tiny as ants. "But this won't be one of those stories."

I ask how.

"They barely scratch the surface. The reporter spends a week, two at most, traveling from one small town to another, never staying more than two nights in one place. In each town he talks with perhaps a dozen people, from the mayor to the old geezer passing time outside the hardware store. When he's seen what he thinks he needs to see he drives his rental car to the nearest airport, hops on a flight home, and writes his story. It's not a bad story. It gives the big picture. And the geezer provides local color. It starts on page one in the Sunday edition and jumps to a page or two inside, with pictures of the mayor and the geezer, a main street with half the storefronts boarded up, railroad tracks with weeds between the ties. Some people read it, at least in part. And when they're done they shake their heads and mutter to themselves, 'Too bad.'

"That's all they say: 'Too bad.' Then they move on to the next story, the sports section, the book review, the crossword. They don't pause to think about what they've just read. They don't ask why a part of our country larger than Texas and California combined is being depopulated as we speak. They don't ask about the people who leave, the ones who stay. Concerning the latter, they never bother to ask why. That's the story that hasn't been reported: why some people defy demographics, laws of economics, even of nature, and stay. That's what we want to find out, tell our readers. And you, Adam, are the one who's going to tell them."

"But why me?" I ask.

Good question. I have no desire to travel to a forlorn hamlet on the high plains, a place stranded by history, sip cold coffee in the local diner while trying to convince the yokel across from me to tell why he stays instead of seeking better prospects elsewhere. I know how long it takes to get folks like him to talk: how tiring, how mindnumbing that is. No matter how long I stay, how many people I talk to, how much they tell me, I cannot report and write a story worthy of the time and money spent to put it together.

It would also be damned inconvenient. My life is here, in the city. I have my favorite wine bar, my places for tapas and sushi. The theater, the museums, the nightspots, the bright lights that never dim, the pulse that never slows: all are mine for the asking. I'll give up none of them for hardship duty in a place people are leaving as quickly as they can start their cars.

And I don't want to leave Petra. For the last year we've shared a loft in a hip part of town. Our relationship is one that takes work to keep going, that cannot be maintained longdistance.

"Can't you give this to someone else?" I ask.

"No. You're the only one who can bring it off."

"You're just saying that."

"You know I wouldn't bullshit you, Adam."

"You've bullshitted me before."

"All right. Maybe I have. But here it is and no bullshit: you've done it before and you can do it again. Can I be more straightforward?"

"No, but—"

"No buts, Adam. You're on this story and that's that. So go in the library and get started on your research. Lost time is wasted time."

That's the editor at his worst: capping off marching orders with a cliché. I have more questions (chiefly why, in a time of falling revenues, this story is more important than saving newsroom jobs), but who am I to ask? I don't draw up the budget, set priorities. Those are jobs gladly left to others. I'm happy simply to turn out stories people like to read and (perhaps) glean something out of.

So it's decided: I'm going to Cold River (population 155 and falling). Now I must explain to Petra. I have an idea she won't like what I say.

I'm right. "If that is not one hell of a note," she says in an accent years of living in the States have failed to erase. "So how long will you be gone?"

I lift up my hands and shrug.

"Why can't you say?"

"Because I don't know long it will be."

"So I will not see you for maybe a long time?"

Now I nod.

"Pet, I don't like this any more than you do. But I don't make the decisions."

"I see." But she doesn't see. The anger hasn't left her voice.

"I love you, Pet. You know I do. I'll miss you every second I'm away from you. And I can hardly wait till I'm with you again."

That's what I say. She says she can hardly wait either. But when I get back will she be around to greet me? Will I care?

•

What gets to me is the space. I've never seen so much of it. Back east space is finite: towns crowd towns, buildings crowd buildings, people crowd people. But now, behind the wheel of a Winnebago (no motel exists within miles of Cold River, so the paper sprung for it), all I see is space: wide, open, empty.

Signs of former habitation abound: caved in ruins of farmhouses, shells of rural churches, silos empty of grain. But living breathing humans are hardly to be seen. On the highway (two lanes of asphalt straight like an arrow as far as the eye can see) I encounter only the rare pickup truck coming toward me, headed for—where? I neither know nor care. My goal is to reach Cold River, get to know place and people so I can return to the city and (perhaps) Petra.

•

I arrive in time for breakfast. Among the businesses still open is the Railroad Café. A throwback, that name: the railroad tracks were torn up thirty years ago. But the name endures. Folks are used to it. Change it, and they'll be upset. It's another dusty storefront, the words

RAILROAD CAFE

carelessly daubed in yellow on the window. Interior décor is nonexistent. Tables and chairs of assorted types and in varied stages of disrepair scattered about a linoleum floor worn down in into pools of black gunky nothingness. On one wall a calendar (hung crooked of course), previous month still displayed. Along another wall a counter, stuffing bursting from each stool. It's not much. It's not even less. But maybe I can get something to eat.

Business is lighter than light. A wizened man, chin unshaved, mouth drawn in for lack of teeth, finishes a meal of fried eggs and homefries and sausage cakes cut up and mashed into a disgusting slop. With a crust of bread he mops up the remains. At another table two men (younger but not by much) linger over coffee. Now and then one of them utters a word. A little later the other responds. I take a table alongside the wall. After a few minutes (ungodly long given lack of trade) a woman, tall and well set up, raw of bone and leery of look, gray hair pulled tightly into a knot atop her head, steely eyes no more than dots in a large wide face, walks over. She takes her time. In a nasal voice that hits my ears like a buzzsaw cutting into a block of wood she asks what I want.

"Can I see a menu?" I ask.

"Aint got one."

"Why don't you?"

"Cause I know what all my customers want."

"What about people passing through?"

"Don't get none."

"None?"

"Nope."

"How come?"

"Hardly a soul comes through n those't do don't stop."

"I see."

"So what's it gonna be?"

I ask for poached eggs with wheat toast and coffee.

"All I got's fried eggs n white bread."

"Seriously?"

"It's what folks eat here. No use offerin somethin if nobody's gonna eat it."

Makes sense, in a way. Even I get it. I change my order to fried eggs and white toast. She doesn't ask if I want my eggs up or over. After another long wait the eggs arrive. They're up and they're good and are accompanied by four slices of toast, plenty of butter on the side. I eat heartily. When I finish I signal the woman. She takes her time getting to my table.

"Can I have my check, please?"

"Aint no check."

Again I ask why.

"Cause everybody eats here knows what t' pay."

"But I don't."

"All right." Some mental arithmetic, then: "Dollar n seventyfive cents."

"Is that all?" Back in the city a plate of eggs with toast and a cup of coffee runs ten dollars or more.

"I usually charge three dollars but seein you didn't have no meat n potatoes I'm only chargin a dollar n seventyfive cents."

I hand her two one dollar bills.

"I'll go get your change."

"No. Keep it."

"I don't take tips."

This time I don't ask. I might not believe the answer.

The woman returns with the quarter. I accept it. But I intend to put it on the table when I leave.

"Are you the only waitress here?"

"Yup. I'm also the cook n the dishwasher. And every afternoon after closin time I wipe down the tables, sweep the floor."

From the looks of the floor she did a cursory job of sweeping yesterday.

"Doesn't the boss help?"

"You're lookin at her. I own the place."

"Well then, I'm pleased to meet you. I'm Adam Keene."

For the first time she smiles: not much but at least not the scowl I'd reckoned was engraved on her face.

"N I'm pleased t' meet you too, Mr Keene. So where you headed for?"

"Right here."

The smile vanishes, the scowl returns.

"You mean you're stayin a while?"

I nod.

"For how long?"

"For as long as it takes for me to finish what I came here to do."

I reach into my wallet, pull out a business card and hand it to her. She looks it over, takes her time. The scowl deepens.

"Well, Mr Keene, I seen your kind before."

"I'm not one of them."

"Then what the devil are you?"

"What the card says I am. And my newspaper sent me here to find out all there is to know about Cold River."

"That's what they all say."

"But I won't be here for just a day or two. I'm staying for as long as it takes to get the story and get it right. So you'll be seeing me around."

"That a fact?"

"It sure is."

I extend my hand. After a while she shakes it.

"Ethel. Ethel Pflug. But everybody's calls me Tiny."

"That's an odd name for a woman."

"It is. But they been callin me that ever since I was little. I was always big for my age, so they called me Tiny cause I was anything but. Even after I got married my husband (God rest his soul) called me Tiny. Me n him bought the restaurant fortyfive years ago n ran it together, then after he passed I kept it goin. Sometimes I wonder why."

"How do you stay open?"

A laugh, grim. "By the hardest. Bus'ness sure aint what it was, but enough still come in for me t' pay the bills n keep body n soul together. So I'll hang on long's I'm fit n able. Besides, what else'm I gonna do with my time?"

"You have a point."

"Now gettin back to folks callin me Tiny: not only so they call me nothin else, it's all they call the restaurant too. They don't call it the Railroad Café, they call it Tiny's. 'We're headin over to Tiny's,' they'll say. Or maybe 'See you at Tiny's': never 'See you at the Railroad Café' but 'See you at Tiny's'. Always Tiny's, never nothin else."

All of a sudden Tiny is a mountain of information. The transformation astounds. I wonder what more I'll learn from her in days to come.

"So where you stayin?" she asks. "Pickins're slim here."

I point to the Winnebago parked in front of the restaurant.

"That yours?" she says.

"It's the paper's. They got it for me."

She looks out the window, past the crude lettering, eyes the Winnebago, shakes her head in childlike wonder.

"Don't see them round here. Don't see much a nothin. So you stayin a while, Mr Keene?"

"Like I said, for as long as it takes. And please call me Adam."

"Sure, Adam. N I suppose you're lookin for a place t' park it."

I nod.

"I know just the place you can."

"You do?"

"Yup. Me n my husband ran a campsite back when more folks was comin this way. It wasn't large, just ten spaces, but we did good business. Most nights in summer we was full, turned folks away. It's still there, by my house. Aint been used in years, but I can hook y' up anyway."

"Thank you, Tiny. I appreciate that."

"Aint nothin."

"How much will it cost?"

"I won't charge an arm n a leg, if that's what's worryin you. Closin time's two, so come back then n we'll go out n hook you up." A pause, then: "Better get busy on lunch. Gettin t' be that time."

And it's time for me to acquaint myself with Cold River, my home (like it or not) for the foreseeable future.

●

My tour is brief. Cold River, the seat of Fowler County, consists of twelve blocks with three streets crossed by four avenues. Fowler Street has what there is of a business district. Railroad Street to the south paralleled the railroad tracks before they were torn up. The only sign of life is the grain elevator, its activity a shadow of old times. Academy Street is north of Fowler. As its name suggests, the schoolhouse is there, so are the churches: Lutheran, Methodist, Catholic. The Catholic church closed years ago, the Lutherans and the Methodists soldier on. The avenues are numbered from east to west. They are residential, the houses on the blocks north of Fowler larger and in better repair than those to the south.

The school is the most imposing building, constructed of red brick and two stories high with a full basement. It houses grades from kindergarten through senior year and serves the entire county, children being few and becoming fewer. There is talk of closing the school, busing the children to Epworth in Satterfield County to the east. Apart from the school, the public buildings bulk puny. The original courthouse burned years ago when struck by lightning during an afternoon storm. Its replacement is a low flatroofed structure of yellow brick that could be mistaken for a veterinary clinic. Cold River's town hall is even less impressive: narrow with room only for a door and a window scarcely wide enough to contain the town's name. It began life as a bank that went bust during the depression; now it suffices for the town clerk, Cold River's only employee, to do her job.

And there is the river. It rises to the west, runs through its namesake town, generally (but not always) between Fowler and Railroad streets. It looks more a creek, so shallow you can see its bed; in drought years it becomes a trickle inching along naked pebbles. But it plays tricks. Following winters of heavy snows or sudden cloudbursts of a summer afternoon it threatens the wellbeing of Cold River and its citizens as much as the tornadoes that roar in with little or no warning.

All this I've learned from hours of research, the rest by a walk lasting not a half hour. I know the facts about Cold River, have seen what I must. Now is the hard part: getting to know its people.

●

When I return to Tiny's I see her joined by a woman of middle years and medium height, attractive with high cheekbones beneath brown eyes set nicely apart: eyes that look into not at you. She's all business, down to ashblond hair gathered into a bun, white blouse and charcoal pants clothing a body that catches a man's eye and keeps it. It catches mine.

Tiny makes introductions. The woman's name is Laura Novotny. She's the principal of Cold River School, teaches English and social studies to the handful of high school students there. And she's happy to meet me.

"Tiny tells me you're planning a different kind of story," she says in a voice as strictly business as her appearance.

"Yes ma'am." (Although not many years younger—ten years, most likely less—I still call her ma'am. Her demeanor demands it.)

"I'm so glad. People need to know that some of us find reason to live here. The reporting thus far has been so negative."

"I agree, Ms Novotny." I see no wedding ring, opt for the neutral.

"Please call me Laura."

"And I'm Adam."

"Adam, I would very much like for us to chat."

"Likewise. What time works for you?"

"Why don't you come by my house for dinner, let's say tomorrow at six?"

"Be glad to."

At last, a smile. "Great. I'll be looking for you. There's so much to talk about and my office is so tiny, not conducive for conversation."

"I look forward to it, Laura."

With a nod of the head and not another word, she leaves the restaurant. Tiny looks at me and smiles. "We better get to the campsite, set y' up," she says.

We do. But my thoughts are of Laura Novotny. There's more to her than meets the eye. But what? That's for me to find out. And, tomorrow night, I will.

•

That evening I phone Petra: easier said than done. Cold River is the deadest of deadzones. I walk about the campsite for what seems an hour before finding a spot that works. I press a button on my phone, hear ringing on the other end.

No pickup: she must be out. Or has switched off her phone. I leave a message, saying I got here and I love her, hope to be back soon. Later, before going to bed, I try again. But still no answer.

My first day in Cold River ends with a sigh. But not because Petra doesn't answer. No: because all I can do is sigh. Not wonder where she may be. Just sigh.

•

My second day is spent among people a reporter talks with: the mayor and town clerk of Cold River, the Fowler County clerk, the sheriff, other leading lights I'm able to track down. The chairman of the board of supervisors is on his ranch in the northern end of the county, so my interview with him must wait another day.

All are pleased to share information, save for the chairman of the board of education, Rodney Haupt, whom I met in his hardware store in Fowler Street: a man slightly past midway in life, receding hairline and moonface unremarkable but for a wen on his upper lip, When I ask about the fate of Cold River School, he answers with fidgety smile: "I'm the chairman a the board; I gotta preside over the meetin, so I shouldn't be expressin my opinion, don't you think? Gotta remain impartial, you know." There's little I can do. He won't talk and that's that. I must query someone else: Laura Novotny, perhaps.

They're nice people: open, friendly. Even Rodney Haupt is cordial. All but he are happy to talk. As is true of many local officials, they talk too much, say little I don't already know. If I'm to learn what makes the people of Cold River tick, I must look elsewhere.

●

My search ends on the steps to the postoffice. There I make the acquaintance of Professor Oscar F (for Frank) Lugenbeel.

He is of average height and bony, strands of white hair combed over a bald pate, watery gray eyes behind rimless spectacles, rabbitlike teeth brown from decades of smoking: a quite looking man whom none would give a second look.

But there's his style of dress. Men hereabouts go for jeans and checked shirts, rancher hats, boots on their feet. But not Professor Lugenbeel. For him it's a loud Hawaiian shirt and Bermuda shorts baring knobby knees, spindly legs. He wears Birkenstocks and no socks, cracked toenails bare for all to see. He looks at home not on the high plains but in a retirement community somewhere in Florida.

But (he says, allowing me not one word) he was born and reared in Cold River, in a onestory frame house with a wide porch out front, smaller one in back, on the right side of Second Avenue, north of Fowler. After (he is not shy to tell) an illustrious career, spanning four decades, teaching English literature at a respected university back east, he has returned to native soil to pass his remaining years in the house in which he spent his formative ones: life coming full circle.

"Young man," he says, air of condescension perfected during long years in the lecture hall, "you have chosen a most propitious moment to arrive."

I ask why. He gladly explains: the Fowler County board of education has been making noise (loudly of late) about shuttering the school. The facts say it all: enrollment has fallen to fortytwo students, with one child entering the first grade come September. Better to bus the children to Epworth, where the school is larger, course offerings more varied. It makes perfect sense. But not to Professor Lugenbeel. "A dreadful idea," he says. "An abomination."

"But the statistics—"

He cuts me off.

"Damn the statistics. You can cook them to suit any purpose you wish. That school is dear to me. My sainted mother taught there. I attended primary school and high school there. I acquired my love of learning there. I prepared for the state university there. But enough of selfish sentiment. As you may have learned, this county takes in a large expanse, its people are widely scattered. Even now, with a school in the county, some children travel long distances each schoolday. If they are forced to go to Epworth, they will be required to leave their homes before dawn, not to return till past dusk. They will spend more hours aboard a bus than in the classroom: one reason why this proposal is such an outrage. But not the most important one." I need not ask. He tells me: "That school is the heart of the community. Take it away and Cold River will perish. And that is gospel truth."

As he talks a thought occurs. Tonight I dine with Laura Novotny. It's her school the powers seek to close. Surely she is against: should the school shut down she'll be out of a job. Is this why she was so quick to invite me? No doubt.

"Young man, I leave you now," Professor Lugenbeel says. He has yet to collect his mail. Perhaps he has forgotten, so intent has he been on unloading his views on me. "But I shall speak with you further. You will be with us for a while, will you not?"

I tell him I will.

●

I rap on the front door of Laura Novotny's house, very like the one Professor Lugenbeel once called and again calls home, but a block west in Third Avenue. The woman who greets me is nothing like the severe schoolmarm I met at Tiny's. Charcoal pants and white blouse give way to tight jeans, peasant shirt baring finely sculpted shoulders and a slender graceful neck. Hair liberated from its bun flows loose and free. Her face, elegant in structure, is scarcely wide enough for the smile she beams. "Hi," she chirps. "C'mon in."

The livingroom is small but well furnished: comfortable chairs, sofa, tables and lamps situated to provide light but not too much of it, TV set discreetly in a corner. Against a wall sits a low bookcase, more books on top, brass horses doing duty as bookends. Above them is a painting. It is of the plains. They don't look as I see them: flat and lifeless, unchanging, beaten down by the sun, blown away by wind. Open land ripples, each ripple a different shade of brown and green and yellow; sky shifts from the palest of blue to purple black. It's a striking piece of art. I want to know who painted it. But later. First I ask, "Is it just us?"

"Afraid so. I invited Professor Lugenbeel. Have you met him?" I nod. She smiles. "But he said there were some Humphrey Bogart movies he wanted to watch. So it's just the two of us. You mind?"

"Not at all." But I wonder: did she invite the good professor knowing he'd beg off, planned instead a cozy tête à tête? Looks suspiciously so.

"Great. Can I get you something to drink? I have wine, but if you prefer something stronger I can offer you a Martini. Would you like a Martini?"

"Yes please."

"I should warn you: it's been a while since I've made one. This isn't Martini country."

"I'll take my chances."

She goes to the kitchen, returns shortly, bearing Martinis full to the brim.

"Thought I'd have one too," she says as she hands me my drink. I take a sip. It's good, quite good. Laura Novotny keeps on surprising.

She joins me on the sofa, sits alongside me: so close I sense the warmth of her body, the scent of her perfume. They do not overpower, instead invite, arouse. I inch closer. She doesn't edge away. Flashes another smile, lets out a tiny laugh. "So tell me, Adam," she says, "what have you learned about our little town?"

"Not as much as I need to know."

"Oh? And what do you need to know?"

"Everything about Cold River and the people who live here."

"Everything?"

"That's what my editor sent me here to do."

"Even everything about me?"

"Yes even about you. So tell me, Laura Novotny: why do you stay?"

"Because it's home. My roots are here. I was born here. I was raised here. My parents, my grandparents are buried here. I've spent almost my entire life here. I love the land, love the people, love living here, breathing the fresh air. I can't imagine any other place I'd want to live. Can you think of better reasons?"

"No." I finish my Martini. She asks if I want another. I do, ask if she minds. Not one bit, she says. And gives a smile not the least faked. When she comes back, drink in hand, I get down to business: "What's this about the school?"

This time there's no smile for me. Mouth tightens, face turns solemn.

"They want to shut it down."

"Can they?"

"If a majority of the board of education votes in favor."

"Would they?"

"Not right now. One's for, one's against. Don't know about Rodney Haupt. He hasn't said."

"I asked him. He said he can't comment."

"And that's because he's the chairman so he has to remain neutral, right?"

"That's about it."

"You do your homework."

"I try." I laugh and so does she. "So it's up in the air—"

"We'll find out next Tuesday."

"That's when they vote."

"Man you're sharp. Yep. That's when."

"How do you feel?"

"I'm against it."

"I suspected as much. Why?"

"It's bad for the children."

"The school in Epworth has more to offer."

"It does. But they'll be spending too much time getting there and back."

"That's what Professor Lugenbeel says."

"He's right."

"But aren't you also thinking about yourself?"

"No."

"You'll lose your job—"

"One of the principals at Epworth is retiring. I'd get her job."

"But you don't want the school to close—"

"No. I don't." She gets up. "Better see about dinner."

As she does I savor my second Martini until the last drop.

●

She serves roasted chicken in Marsala sauce, wild rice and grilled asparagus. A bottle of wine sits on the table. Laura pours for me, then herself. I dig in.

"This is good," I tell her. "Very good."

"Not what you were expecting in Cold River, huh?"

"No. My eating experience here's been confined to Tiny's—and what I fix for myself in the Winnebago. You can imagine what that's like."

She laughs. "Sure can."

"But this? This is a real treat. How'd you do it?"

"I like to cook. But I rarely get a chance to show off."

"Then I came along—"

More laughter. "Yes. You came along."

"Where'd you learn?"

"I lived in Denver for a while, after college. My husband and I ate out a lot and I picked up ideas."

"So there's a husband?"

"There was."

"What happened?"

"We divorced. I was homesick, wanted to come back here, and he didn't. That's one reason why we split."

I wonder what the others may be. She doesn't say, I don't ask. She's an honest woman. If she wants to tell she will. But later: the time is not ripe for sharing secrets. She has hers. And I have mine.

●

After dessert (chocolate sauce over vanilla ice cream) we retire to the livingroom, to the sofa. Once more we are close. Very close. The conversation picks up again.

"So Novotny's your married name?" I say.

"My maiden name. I began using it again after the divorce."

I ask why.

"I'm proud of my name. My people were among the first settlers in what's now Fowler County. They were Czech."

"I didn't know Czechs settled here."

"Haven't you read Willa Cather?"

I have not. She explains about My Ántonia. It rings a bell, nothing more.

Now a smile. "There's something else I want you to know."

"I'm all ears."

She has nothing to say, places her lips on mine, begins kissing. One thing leads to another until she gets up, takes me into her bedroom. It has a double bed in which (if I were to guess) she has slept alone for longer than she'd care to admit.

On that bed Laura Novotny and I become lovers.

●

So that's it, I tell myself, hours later but still awake. That's why she invited me. She didn't want to talk about the school. She wanted to get laid.

She knew (and still knows) next to nothing about me, and I knew (and still know) next to nothing about her. But we made love—and enjoyed it.

This is a first for me, bedding a news source. It's not unheard of. A female war correspondent was famous for sleeping with generals in hope of a scoop. Sometimes she got one. But I wasn't after a scoop, just good food, good company: a pleasant evening away from the Winnebago.

That I got—and more. And from a woman who gave herself in the most generous and loving way I've ever known.

•

Before falling asleep, another thought: I never got around to asking who painted the picture on the livingroom wall.

•

Later, waking in black predawn darkness: I didn't phone Petra. Worse: I don't wonder where she might be, what she might be doing. That's bad.

•

It's Professor Lugenbeel's turn to play host. From the outside his house resembles Laura's. But step inside and similarities end. Laura's house has a look of being lived in. Professor Lugenbeel lives on display. An oriental rug covers the livingroom floor, fringes lined up like soldiers on parade. Not a speck of dust is visible on the round walnut table next to the winged chair the good Prof favors while entertaining guests. On the coffee table (also free of dust) books are neatly stacked, largest on the bottom, smallest on top. In place of a painting that comes straight from the heart are framed prints from pages of English satirical reviews of an earlier century. And instead of a Martini I'm offered Scotch: Glenlivet single malt, a real treat. I have mine on the rocks. Professor Lugenbeel prefers his neat.

"So, Mr Keene, what do you make of our fair burg?" he asks, still at the lectern, hurling questions at students. He may have retired, but he can't give it up.

"It's interesting."

"Is that all you can say—interesting?" He sips Scotch. "Surely you have formed impressions."

"I have."

"And what may they be?"

"I'd rather not say."

"Oh? And why not?"

"I've been here only a few days. That's hardly time to form an opinion."

"A clever answer."

"Thank you, Professor."

"It is not intended as a compliment."

"It's not?"

"Certainly not. One cannot sit on the sidelines, making notes. One must enter the debate."

"Then you're part of the story. You can't report it objectively."

"Indeed you are clever."

"No I'm a journalist. And a journalist's job is not to participate."

He drinks more Scotch. This time he has more than a sip.

"Balderdash. Tommyrot. Utter hypocrisy. You journalists break your damn rules all the time." Allowing not a nanosecond for me to respond, he goes on: "You participate in every story you report. And do not attempt to deny that. When I open a newspaper I see bias on every page, in every column, every paragraph and sentence. You inject opinion without shame. You may not think you do. You may even believe that you are objective. And why not? You see yourself: through the prism of your peculiar worldview, the way you were taught to see. I know that worldview well. I saw it on campus all the time."

He pours Scotch into his glass, doesn't ask if I'd like my drink freshened. I use the pause to say, "Professor Lugenbeel, what's the purpose of this harangue?"

"It is no such thing."

"But that's how it comes off."

"That is not my intention. But I am a man of strong opinions."

"So I've noticed."

"And I am not hesitant to voice them. I never have been, I am not now and I never will be until I draw my last gasp—which will be some while away."

I wonder what makes him so confident of a long life. But (I suppose) he will allow himself nothing less.

"There's nothing wrong with that," I tell him.

"Of course there's not. 'There can be no progress without the clash of minds.' Jefferson said that, in case you are not aware—"

"I am."

"Good. Glad to hear that. Some minds of course are superior to others."

"And yours is one of them, I'm sure."

"By God, for a young man you are good."

"I'm not as young as I used to be." Younger though than Laura, by as much as a decade. But not too young to want her. I want her right now, want to make love to her instead of listening to Professor Lugenbeel run on.

He pours more Scotch. This time he asks if I'd like some. I do.

"To change the subject," he says, "I understand that Mrs Novotny has had you to dinner."

"She has." I wonder how he knows. Wonder also what more he knows. Wonder why I didn't think he would know.

"An admirable woman. She fights the good fight. And has placed herself among the angels. I wish her Godspeed."

"But will she prevail?"

"That is the question. Surely people in this county support her cause. I cannot imagine why they would not. But do they support it strongly enough? Will they step forward and fight? I wonder. By the bye, have you met her daughter?"

"She has a daughter?" That's a bolt out of the blue. Not once has Laura mentioned children.

"Indeed so. And (I fear) of a very different stamp."

I ask how.

"Firstly she intends to educate her child herself and not in public school."

"A child too?" Laura has said nothing about a grandchild either. My evening with Professor Lugenbeel, until now tedious, suddenly proves enlightening.

"Yes. A boy. He must be three by now, but I have seen neither he nor his mother of late. You see, she comes to town only to purchase supplies and even that is seldom. She stocks up for months, it seems."

"What's her name?"

"Echo."

"Pretty."

"But a bit odd, I daresay. And the name of her son is stranger still."

"And what's that?"

"Earth."

"That's his name—Earth?"

"Just so."

"That is different."

"An odd young woman, Echo Novotny. Very odd indeed."

"What does she do?"

"She is an artist of some sort."

"Where does she live?"

"Way out in the country. She sees nobody, nobody sees her."

"Not even her mother?"

"I would have no idea. Mrs Novotny does not say whether she and her daughter communicate. Come to think of it, she rarely speaks of her daughter. Rarely utters a word."

"Very interesting."

"Indeed."

●

"Why didn't you tell me you have a daughter?" I ask Laura. Once more we're in her bed, once more we've made love, once more it was good. The passion she brings makes up for her lack of imagination. "And why didn't you tell me she lives here in the county, and has a son, your own grandchild?"

My question takes her by surprise. It's not postcoital smalltalk. It has an edge. Her voice, heretofore dozy and content, changes abruptly.

"Who told you?" she says, agitated.

"Professor Lugenbeel. He had me over for drinks."

"I don't talk much about my daughter."

I try not to badger, but: "Why not?"

"We're different people. But I love her and in her own way she loves me."

"Professor Lugenbeel says she's an artist."

"She is. And she's brilliant."

"What kind of art does she do?"

"She paints."

"Where can I see her work?"

"You already have, probably."

"Where?

"In the livingroom."

"You mean that painting?"

"Yes."

"I thought you'd bought it somewhere."

"No. She painted it just for me."

"She did?"

"Yes. She knows how much I love this county. Nobody'd ever done a painting with a Fowler County setting and she thought I'd like it."

"And you did—"

"Very much. She couldn't have done anything nicer for me."

"I agree. It's unique: the colors, the bold strokes, the rippling effect. It's perhaps the most wonderful painting I've ever seen."

"Seriously?"

"I've never seen anything like it. Best thing is it comes straight from the heart. You should be very proud of her, Laura."

"I am." She smiles. In the darkness I see it on her face. "And thank you. That means a lot to me."

She gives a kiss, we embrace. For the second time tonight we make love. As before it's good, better perhaps. Then we talk: things a man and a woman say in the afterglow of sex. None of it concerns her daughter. But she's still on my mind. I have seen the painting. Now I must meet the artist.

●

Tiny brings fried eggs and toast and coffee. This time I order sausage cakes and potatoes too.

"Findin everything you need t' know?" she asks as I mop up egg yolk with a scrap of toast.

"Yes and no."

"What you mean?"

"Means yes I'm finding out things and no, I still need to find out more."

"I'd call that progress."

"You do?"

"Yup. Takes a while t' get t' know folks here."

"So I've learned. But I'm getting to know some of them too well."

"Like who?"

"Professor Lugenbeel."

Tiny lets out a whoop so loud it probably is heard in every corner of the state. And this state, unlike the ones back east, is big and wide open.

"Aint hard gettin your fill a him," she says. "He's a talker."

"Smart man though."

"Maybe too smart. Aint a thing that man don't know. But he got it all from readin books. When it comes t' life there's some things he's gotta learn."

"He doesn't think much of Laura Novotny's daughter."

"Echo?" Another whoop. "Known her since she was little. She's different, that's for sure. But she does love this county. She truly does. So Oscar was goin off against Echo—"

"Among other things."

"He shouldn't be callin her strange. He's peculiar too, always has been. Now don't get me wrong. We're glad he came back here when he retired. We need all the folks we can get here. But he is an odd one n I don't understand why. His father ran the grain elevator, his mother taught school. Most normal folks y'd ever want t' of met. Echo? She comes by it more honest."

"How so?"

"Her father. Never knew him, never showed his face here. Him n Laura met at the university, got married there, then they split, not long after Echo was born. But from things Laura's said he was somethin of a free spirit, lived his life the way he wanted. Yup. That's where Echo gets it, from her father. Not from Laura. N speakin a Laura, I hear you been spendin time with her."

I ask Tiny how she knows.

"Laura told me. She says she enjoys keepin comp'ny with you."

I ask what she thinks.

"Good thing, I'd say. Heaven knows when she last had a man in her life. So treat her right, Adam. She's a good girl, best there is."

I tell her I will.

"John Novotny was her father. Fine man. So was her grandfather. Charles Novotny. Had one a the best farms in the county n his father Antonin Novotny was the one that built the Catholic church here. Said there was Catholics in the county that needed a church n he built 'em one. That was her grandfather n her great grandfather. N John Novotny was every bit as fine a man. Wasn't a thing he wouldn't do for anybody. Dropped dead of a heart attack while takin food to Flossie Ryan that broke her leg. Yup. Died while tryin to help a fellow human bein. That's the kind a stock Laura's from. So don't you hurt her none."

"I won't."

"Didn't figure you would. But I thought I'd say it anyways. Sounds like you swept her off her feet n she's pretty vulnerable, if you get what I'm sayin."

I get it loud and clear.

●

It's time to meet the other Novotny woman.

To get to her place I borrow Tiny's Jeep; the Winnebago eats too much gas. And the Jeep does better on terrain where a road is nothing more than tire tracks leading across broad plains to a place far beyond the naked eye.

First in view is a dwelling unlike any I've seen. It's not built like others houses here, of wood or (more occasionally) brick, but of stone and it's mostly underground. On the roof are solar panels for heating and cooling, its only concession to modern life. Echo Novotny lives off the land, requires only simple technology, minimal creature comforts.

Then I see her. She must have heard the Jeep, for she rushes out to see who's coming. Her hair, ashblond like her mother's, falls to her waist and below. Her face too is like Laura's, as are her eyes: large and wideset and brown. She's a younger version of her mother, young and pretty. No not pretty: beautiful, strikingly so. She may be the most beautiful woman I've ever seen.

But there's something more, something neither Laura nor Tiny nor Professor Lugenbeel prepared me for. She is naked, completely so—as is her son, a tiny fellow who follows her out of the house. Neither is embarrassed. Just the opposite: she faces me as if it's the normal thing to greet a stranger in the buff.

"Something I can do for you?" she asks, eyes narrowed to a squint.

I identify myself, state my purpose. I also mention the painting, tell her I like it. Tell her it's the most striking piece of art I've ever chanced upon.

"You came out here to tell me that?" She has yet to give her name. I know what it is, but I'd like to hear her say it.

"Yes, but I have other questions too. So will you talk to me?"

Squint goes away, eyes turn pretty again. "Sure."

"I'm sorry. I should've told you I was coming. Here you are, no clothes—"

Eyes now turn mirthful. And a laugh, mirthful also.

"Don't worry about it. I go naked in summer months." She explains how this saves water, keeps animals alive: reasons many environmentally conscious young women might give. But this is the first time I've met one who does what she says.

As she talks I see body hair. Since her hair is light, her skin tanned, it's less noticeable on her legs. But when she raises her arms I see tufts in the pits. Those I cannot pretend away.

"We're about to have lunch," she says. "Would you like to join us?"

I do. The meal consists of chopped tomatoes and peppers lightly grilled and served on flatbread, washed down by herbal tea. We sit at a table that's nothing more than rough boards on a trestle, on benches with no backs.

I gawk at Echo's breasts. I can't help it, they're there to be seen: round and firm, small dark pink areolae ringing taut nipples. She knows I'm looking. But does nothing to stop me, beams a knowing grin that tells me (in ways words can't) it's okay. And who knows? Maybe she likes it. Some women do. And she's not exactly hiding her body from me.

"Everything you're eating was made here," she says. "The tomatoes and peppers were grown in the garden. And I baked the bread this morning."

"I'm impressed."

A shrug. "Anyone can do it. But not many do. It's too easy to get a meal out of a can. Or at the nearest fast food place. I choose to be different. I make healthy food for me and my son. And that's all we eat. Right, Earth?"

The boy smiles. Utters not a word, just giggles. He enjoys his food. At least he eats it, every scrap. That's more than I did at his age. My mother was always on my back about licking my platter clean. Always laying a guilt trip about starving children in Africa who'd gladly eat what I refused. He's also well trained. Though small, he helps his mother clear the table. He can't carry much, only his teacup. But he does his part. And without being told: also more than I did at his age.

Chores done, he takes his nap. Goes to his bed in a corner of an enormous room in which living space and kitchen, sleeping areas and artist's studio all have discrete parts. Private space does not exist. Even the toilet sits in clear view.

"Quite a boy," I tell Echo after he's asleep. We walk through empty silent land surrounding the house, gently rolling as far as I can see.

"I do my best."

"So where's his dad?"

"I don't know. We lost touch. My idea."

"But Earth's his son—"

"He is."

"So he has to care."

"Perhaps."

"I don't get it."

"I wanted a child. I wanted it by him. But I didn't want to marry him. I don't want to marry any man. But I want more children. I've even chosen their names."

I ask what they are.

"Wind, Rain and Fire."

"Unusual names."

"They all fit. Earth, Wind, Rain, Fire: four children, four elements."

"What if some of them are girls?"

"Doesn't matter. I'll name them Wind, Rain and Fire anyway."

"So when will you have another child?"

"When I've found a man I want to have one by."

"But you won't marry him—"

"No. I just want his baby."

●

What's with the plan to have four children named after each of the elements? I wonder. Does she think the human species will soon condemn itself to extinction and she, safe on high plains miles from anywhere, will be the last woman alive? Does she fancy herself a new Eve, mother of a race that will repopulate the planet?

Likely the thought has never crossed her mind. Echo Novotny lives her life as she believes it should be lived. Just like her father (so says Tiny). And unlike others having the same dream, she does that, right here, right now.

●

Next day I'm back. Echo's beauty beckons, makes me want to behold ashblond hair falling below the waist, pretty wideset eyes on broad cheekbones, small body proportioned just right. I want to behold all day.

I'm not here to ask why she stays while others leave. I already know. I knew the minute I learned she'd painted the picture. Knew she loves the land, saw that in the terrain, its contours, how they ripple, shades of yellow and brown and green skillfully blended to make a work of art. A masterpiece.

"So you really like the painting," she says. We sit at the table. Earth is napping, but our talk does not waken him.

"Yes I do. It captures something no camera, not even the human eye, can do. Only one thing can capture that."

"And that is?"

"The heart. That painting comes straight from the heart."

"Go on." She likes what she hears. But others have mouthed these words without meaning them. She wants to make sure I do.

"No creative work—a painting, a sculpture, a piece of music, a novel—is good unless it comes from the heart. Otherwise it's colors slapped onto canvas, odd chippings on stone, noise without feeling, words that convey nothing. That painting comes from the heart and that's what makes it great."

She smiles broadly. "I think you mean it."

"Every word."

She turns quiet. Pensive. Then smiles again.

"Hey. There's something I want you to do."

"Yeah?"

"I want you to—well, you know what I'm talking about."

"I'm not sure I do."

Laughing: "Do I have to draw a map?"

She doesn't. But: "Now?"

"Yes. Now."

My jaw drops. I'm in shock. She can't be serious. But she is.

I give another look, quick but enough for me to know I want her. She walks to her bed, lies down. I remove my clothes and climb atop her.

"Not like that," she says. "The other way, like animals do."

Her wish is my command. I mount her, we begin copulating. She knows how to move her body, respond to mine. Her timing is without fault, as if she anticipates what I'm about to do. But there's no fire, not even a spark. For her it's a coupling, nothing more.

I think of Laura (and oh my God now I've done it, diddling both mother and daughter), how her body is older, less supple, how she makes up for that with feeling, with fire. With heart, with all she has to give. How I wish I were with her and not Echo.

After we're done I look over to see Earth, up from his nap and staring with eyes wide open. "He's been watching us," I say to Echo.

She shrugs. And tells Earth to resume his nap. He does.

"Doesn't that bother you? A little boy watching his mother—"

"He's watched animals do it."

"You mean you don't mind?"

"It's the most natural thing there is, animals mating, and a man and a woman mating is no different."

I give a hard look. "Did you say mating?"

"Yes. You and I are mating."

"We're doing no such thing."

"Yes we are. I want a baby and I've chosen you to give me one."

Once again I'm stunned. Never before has a woman given herself to me so I could furnish sperm: the chosen biological father to a child who, regardless of sex, will be named Wind.

"You could have told me."

"Then you might have said no. And I didn't want you to."

"But why me? And why now?"

"Because the timing is right."

"Timing? What timing?"

"First, I want another baby. And second, I found the man I want to be that baby's father."

"So why me? And when did you decide?"

"When I learned your name."

"My name?"

"Yes. Adam. The first human."

"So that's it. You like my name."

"Yes. It's a very good name. But I had to be absolutely sure you were the right one. Then when you said you liked the picture and I knew you weren't bullshitting me—well, I had no doubt: you would be the father of Wind."

Sarcastic: "I suppose I should be honored."

"You're not mad, are you?"

"Damn right I am."

"I'm sorry."

I ignore her apology. "What makes you so sure we've made a baby?"

"Because it's time."

"Time?"

"I'm ovulating. If one of your sperm—"

Now I get it. The story I'd come to write, the one I thought I knew how to write before I got to Fowler County, has taken a very strange turn.

"So it's just science that makes you choose a man to father your child."

"Not entirely."

"Then what is it?"

"I have to like him, want to be with him. And I wanted to be with you. I like you, Adam. I like you a lot."

"You hardly know me."

"That doesn't matter."

"What does?"

"You give a good vibe. If you didn't I wouldn't have chosen you."

I've heard more than enough. I get off the bed, into my clothes.

"Where are you going?" she asks.

"Back to town."

"Won't you stay for supper?"

"No. I've got to get back now."

That's the truth. I want to get away. Want to forget any of this happened. But I can't. It is with me and will stay with me. What is done is done. And can never be taken back.

●

"What's wrong, sweetie?" Laura asks. She wants to make love. I don't. I shouldn't even be here. "You haven't said a word. So—what's bugging you? Something is. So tell me. Please."

I don't answer. She smiles. I have no idea why.

"I know just the thing to lose those blues," she says and unzips me, performs an act I hadn't figured to be in her repertoire of sexual tricks.

"That was a pleasant surprise," I tell her when she's finished.

"You're the first man I've done that to since my husband. And that was while I still loved him."

Now I feel like crap. But I follow her to bed and make love, not because I want to but because she expects it. And that makes her happy.

But it makes me feel crappier still, more than I've felt in all my life.

●

In the bunk tucked into one side of the Winnebago I remain restless, my mind spawning thoughts I'd rather not think. But I can't avoid avoid thinking, begin talking to myself as if I'm another person.

Talk fatherhood: a job you're not cut out for. But worry not, friend. Echo will do it for you. That's right: Earth Mother, Mother of Earth, will do it all. Will be father as well as mother to Wind. And do a better job than you. For in picking a father, even just a biological one, she couldn't have made a worse choice. You don't know squat about parenting. More: you don't want to know. And you won't have to know, for you'll never see the child. Wind Novotny will grow up not knowing his/her father. That's how his/her mom wants it. All she wants from a man, all she wanted from you, is your seed planted in her. She'll handle the rest.

You didn't ask Echo to have sex. She asked you. You thrust your seed into her, she received it. She didn't love you, certainly you didn't love her, but the two of you might have made a baby. But you'll never know. She won't tell. She'll cast you off, just like the man who provided seed for Earth, the men who will do the same for Rain and Fire. She wants four children, each named for an element. To get them she chooses a man, they copulate, and nine months later the child is born.

What's worse is what you have done to Laura: as true and as honest a woman as you will find. She unlike her daughter hasn't the talent to show her heart on canvas. So she shows it in the way she gives herself to you.

So what have you done? You have rutted (dogs and bitches rut, you were just another dog, Echo another bitch, so be honest: you rutted) with her daughter. You didn't want to, but you did. And now you can't make love to her. Oh you can rut. That's easy. But you cannot make love to her the way she makes love to you. It will not be true, nor will it be honest. You can't give to her what she gives to you. That's what you have done.

And now, tossing restlessly in your bunk in the Winnebago, you gnaw on that bone long and hard. Gnaw long and hard thinking of Echo, thinking of Laura, especially Laura. Gnaw long and hard thinking of what you have done.

What a shitty place this world is. And you're part of it.

●

In my mind I have become so much of a story that I forget the story I'm here to report. My newspaper is forking out a hefty sum for it. It's time for me to earn that money.

Opportunity presents itself on Tuesday night. The county board of education is to decide the fate of Cold River School. I attend by myself. Professor Lugenbeel has invited me to sit with him, but I decline. And I've not asked Laura if she'd like for me to sit with her. For I haven't seen her, have avoided her like a disease.

Fowler County has few people, but many of them appear. The courtroom is tiny, so some must stand. Many, perhaps most, still hope the school will remain open. I'm less certain. But what do I know? I've covered enough meetings such as this. It's like the fat lady singing—

The board members sit at a table beneath the judge's banc, facing the crowd. They're an unimpressive lot, dressed in suits seldom worn, tugging at neckties carelessly knotted around shirtcollars too tight or too loose around the neck. The chairman, Rodney Haupt, sits in the middle. He calls the meeting to order.

Professor Lugenbeel rises. Mr Haupt recognizes him. "You may go ahead, Mr Lugenbeel."

"That is not the correct form of address, Mr Chairman."

Exasperated: "Then what is it?"

"It is Professor Lugenbeel, Mr Chairman, Professor Oscar Frank Lugenbeel. And frankly, sir, I am appalled at your ignorance." (I crane my neck Laura's way, see a pained look on her face. I wish I was with her, but—) "I am a son of this county who has returned after long years of teaching English literature at one of the nation's more distinguished universities. My books on Sterne and Goldsmith are widely regarded as the most authoritative critiques of their works to be published. It astonishes me that you have heard of neither them nor their author."

"I'm sorry, sir, but I never have."

"Of course not. I doubt that you even know who Sterne and Goldsmith are. But believe it as gospel truth when I say that I have been in education since the time you were still in diapers. I know education. I know how it works. Indeed I have forgotten more about education than you or any of your colleagues on this benighted board will ever know."

My God he's drunk too much Scotch, I tell myself, then wonder again what Laura thinks. Funny how my thoughts return to her.

"Well, Professor," Mr Haupt says, "you got something you wanta say?"

"Have I not been saying it?"

"Yes you have. But I'd like t' know exactly what you got t' say on the issue a closin Cold River School. You got anything t' say bout that?"

"Indeed I do. I wish to say that your proposal is one of the most asinine ideas I have ever heard and you are all clods even to propose such a thing."

On he goes, heaping abuse while citing solid facts, making cogent arguments until Mr Haupt tells him his time is up. Mr Haupt asks if others wish to speak. They do. He allows them their say. When the last speaker is finished he calls for a vote. It is two to one. Cold River School will not reopen in the fall.

The meeting is over. Many mill around. I have no wish to stay. As I leave the room I turn and see Laura, alone, tears rushing down her face. I should go over, place my arm around her, say something. But I don't. What can I say, and how?

Sad. How very sad.

●

The story is done: nothing more to do but wrap it up. And leave Cold River.

Two questions remain: (1) what will I tell Laura? and (2) when?

The answers: (1) I don't know and (2) I don't know.

●

"Got a bone t' pick," Tiny says as I sit down for breakfast.

I have no idea of what she's talking about. So I ask.

"Laura," she says. "I don't like what you're doin t' her."

I don't like it either, but I wonder if Tiny means the same thing I mean.

"You been avoidin her, that's what you been doin," she goes on. "She tells me every time she sees you you look the other way. She don't know what she's done t' make you ignore her like that."

It's nothing she's done; it's what I've done. But I can't tell Tiny. She's right, though. I should tell Laura, tell it now. But how can I say, "Hey Laura, guess what? I banged your daughter."

So what can I say? And, right now, what can I tell Tiny?

"I've finished my story," I say at last. "I'm leaving tomorrow."

"And you don't know how t' break it to her, that it?"

"Yeah. That's it." Some of it, at least: the easy part. But still news that will be hard to break.

"Well, you better tell her somethin. She's gonna miss the devil out a you."

"She will?"

95

"Durn right. Don't you know?"

"Know what?"

"That woman's stuck on you. Man she's stuck on you bad."

"Oh shit."

"So get yourself over there n tell her best you can. Tell her you're gonna miss her like crazy. N tell her right now. Time's wastin."

"All right, Tiny. I'll go as soon as I've eaten my breakfast."

"No y'aint. You're goin right now. I aint servin you till you seen her."

But how can I put together words when I still don't know what those words are? How can I tell Laura she did the worst thing she could have done: fall for me?

I get up, resigned to the moment. But as I start out the door, the siren atop the firehouse begins wailing. I don't know what that means. But Tiny does. "Get back inside," she barks.

"What for?"

"Just get back in here n follow me t' the bathroom."

I do as she says. In the bathroom (which is none too clean) she orders me to crouch on the floor, facing the inside wall. I do as she says.

"What's this all about?" I ask.

"Tornado's comin. That's what."

No sooner do the words leave her mouth than I hear, drawing closer with each second, a fearsome noise like a train roaring past at full speed, only louder, more deafening: a noise I never want to hear again. As it gets louder, accompanied by sounds of things crashing and smashing, I huddle in fear I haven't felt before: fear I can't describe. I haven't prayed in years, have forgotten how, but I try. Try to pray that when the tornado passes Tiny and I (and Laura) are still alive, unharmed.

As swiftly as it came the tornado is gone. Tiny rises to her feet. So do I. She opens the door. The restaurant is a shambles, tables upside down, front window with its crudely lettered words now bits of glass strewn about the floor. But the building is still in one piece. The same can't be said for others. Two doors down Clyde Rupp's barbershop (open Tuesdays and Saturdays 10 to 5) is rubble. With capricious design the tornado has spared some buildings, leveled others. As I look down the street the sight resembles a warzone.

The same is true for the rest of Cold River. Apart from roof damage Laura's house is unscathed, but in the driveway her Ford Explorer sits mortally wounded, tree toppled on top of it. A block to the east Professor Lugenbeel's home is a jumble of wood and masonry and flotsam such as his oriental rug and his favorite armchair. Cold River School is a pile of bricks, not a wall intact. Never, anywhere, have I seen such destruction.

Before anything else, even checking on Tiny's house or the Winnebago, we knock on Laura's front door. There's no answer.

"That's funny," Tiny says. "Her car's here n from the looks of it she can't go nowhere in it."

"Means she's got to be here somewhere. Let's try again."

Once more we knock. Still no response. Tiny opens the door (unlocked: you can still do that here), shouts Laura's name once, twice, even a third and fourth time, all to no avail. "I got an idea where she may be," she says. "N it don't make me too hopeful."

"Where?"

"Leave that t' me. I got a job for you."

I ask what.

"Goin out t' Echo's n tellin her there's been a tornado n her mom's missin."

I'd endure ten root canals before that. "Can't you call her?"

"Don't know if she got a phone n if she does I aint got the number."

There is no phone. Echo's back to nature mindset precludes technology.

"So how am I going to get out there?" I ask.

"Let's go see bout that."

We walk to Tiny's house. It has escaped the worst. But there's no sign of the Winnebago. "Looks like the twister up n dumped it," Tiny says.

"Where?"

"Can't say. Could be anywhere: next field, half mile, mile, two miles away."

She doesn't say, but it comes to mind anyway: had I been in the Winnebago I'd be dead now. The thought will give me shudders for as long as I live.

"There's no way I can get out to Echo's."

"You can use the Jeep. It wasn't harmed."

"So why don't you go yourself?"

"Too much t' do here."

"Then I ought to stay here and help."

"You wouldn't know what t' do. I been through this before, know what's gotta get done. So get out there n tell Echo."

"But I want to help find Laura."

"There'll be enough people doin that. So get your butt out there now."

I get.

●

Echo waits outside when I arrive. She must have heard me coming: sound travels far here. She is, as usual, naked.

"Didn't expect to see you again," she says, half smiling.

"I have news. And I'm afraid it's not good." As I tell her the half smile vanishes, pretty brown eyes turn down. Tears form in ducts, trickle down cheeks.

"Oh my God," she groans. And groans again. Then: "Is she gonna be okay?"

"I don't know. That's why you've got to come to town."

"Let me round up Earth and get some clothes on us."

"Pack a bag. Food and water too. You could be there a while."

"Sure, sure. I'll be right back."

She is, fully clothed in checked shirt and bluejeans. Earth is dressed in teeshirt and shorts. They get into Echo's all terrain vehicle. Earth asks, "Mama, we going somewhere?"

"We're going to see Gran Gran."

"We are?"

"Yes. Something's happened and we have go to town and see if she's okay."

"I hope she is, Mama."

"I hope she is too, sweetie. Oh God I do, I do."

Echo follows as I push the old Jeep as fast and as hard as it can go over a road that's no more than two tracks of tire marks so faint I must keep my eyes glued lest end up miles from Cold River. Yes wrecked Cold River where Echo and I (and, as much as his young mind can reckon, Earth) hope Laura is alive and well.

Hope. That's all we have. Hope that Laura will be found alive and I can say goodbye, leave Cold River with something like a clear conscience.

•

When we reach town Tiny has news.

"We just found Laura. She was at the school." She looks at Echo, not me. "Echo honey, I sure hate tellin you this, but your mother didn't make it through."

"You mean she's dead?" Echo says in a high short gasp.

Tiny nods sadly. Echo burst into tears. Earth, seeing his mother, cries also. And although I can't remember when I last cried, I join them.

"She must of been there when it hit." Tiny's eyes are shot with blood, as if she's had a cry. As she tells the news tears return. "I had an idea she might of been there, so I went up right away, took some rescue people with me. One a them seen an arm danglin from where her office use t' be n they started diggin. Didn't take long t' pull her out." She throws up her hands. "That's where she was—in her office. If only I could figure out why—"

Several possibilities arise. Laura may have getting things together to take to her new position at Epworth. Or she'd decided not to take the job and was clearing out her stuff. Or was it something else? We'll never know. She'd heard the siren, knew it was coming. But in the seconds she had to get to safety she stayed where she was. And why? I think I know the answer. It's not one I like.

Echo cries a storm. I leave her to her grief. I have my own to deal with. It's more than coming to grips with the loss of someone who has come into my life, who means more to me than I'd imagined. Laura is dead because of what I did—and did not do. She is dead because of me.

•

We're allowed to view the corpse. It's not a pretty sight. The body is crushed in places, the skull bashed in. Now there is no doubt: Laura is dead.

We look, Echo and Tiny and I. Echo sheds more tears. So do I.

"Why?" I ask. "Why, Laura? Why'd you stay? Tell me: why?"

But she doesn't answer. She can't. She's dead.

•

But Professor Lugenbeel is alive. For a while folks thought he was dead, buried in the rubble of his house. But later he showed up, having driven to the liquor store at Epworth to stock up on Scotch. He returned to find himself without a home but with plenty of Glenlivet with which he can drink away his troubles.

Professor Lugenbeel is alive and Laura is dead. And all because of where they were. If they'd been in their homes he would be dead and she'd be alive. But they weren't, so he is alive and she's dead. Funny how that is. No, not funny. Not funny at all.

•

I phone the paper to tell what happened, ask if they want a story.

"Nah," the editor on duty says. Though we work for the same employer I recognize neither voice nor name. "We'll get it off the AP."

"But I'm right here. I know the town, know the people. The person who was killed was—uh yes she'd become a friend. I saw it happen, saw it with my own eyes. I can provide color the AP won't have. So do you want it?"

"Nah. We'll stick with the AP. It's only worth a graf or two—if that."

He hangs up, doesn't even thank me for calling. Just a click, then a dialtone.

No wonder newspapers are going out of business.

•

Echo sits on the porch. Her eyes, red from tears, stare across the street. At what? I have no idea. Likely neither does she. She sits and stares. Shakes her head, stares some more. Says not a word, just stares.

Earth sits alongside her. He knows something has happened. He asks his mother. She doesn't answer, just stares.

I sit at her other side. If I'd never laid eyes on her Laura might still be alive. But I smile anyway. She's just lost her mother. I know what that's like. And my mother wasn't killed by a tornado. The family knew she would die long before she did. We grieved. But we weren't plagued by whys and ifs. Echo is.

At last she says: "Why?" And then: "Why'd she do it? Why'd she go to the school?"

"We'll never know," I tell her. I do know, but I won't tell Echo. I won't tell anyone. I'll keep it deep within me, where even I won't find it.

"No. I suppose not." She pauses. "You liked her, didn't you?"

"Liked who?"

"Mom. You liked her."

Silence.

"She liked you. Tiny said she did."

"What does Tiny know?"

"Mom told her. She liked you, Adam. She even thought she loved you."

Again, silence.

"You and Mom did it, right?"

More silence.

"That's what Tiny said. Mom told her you two slept together."

I break my silence: "Do you believe her?"

"Yeah. You did. I know you did."

"What makes you so sure?"

"I'm a woman. Women know these things."

"Okay. We did. Does that upset you?"

"No. I'm happy, actually. Mom was lonely. She needed someone."

"And I just happened to be the one that was there."

"It was more than that. A whole lot more. She loved you, Adam."

"We hardly knew each other."

"Sometimes that happens. It just does."

"Yeah. You're a woman. You know that shit."

"You really hate me, don't you?"

It's the truth. But I don't want to tell her. She may be the mother of my child—whom I will never know.

"I don't blame you. I was the one that messed everything up."

"Maybe."

"Don't bullshit me, Adam. After—well, after what we did you didn't want to face her. You couldn't face her."

"You're right. What's worse, I was about to tell her I was leaving when the tornado hit. I never had a chance to say goodbye."

"That must hurt."

"It does."

"So you really did love her."

"Maybe. Maybe I did."

●

The funeral is scheduled for Monday. I don't want to remain in Cold River another minute but delay my departure. I couldn't say goodbye, but I can honor her memory. That's the least I can do.

Until then I need a place to sleep. The Winnebago is scattered in pieces strewn up to a mile from the campsite. Tiny would take me in, but her house is up to the rafters with folks whose homes were destroyed or damaged. I'll have to sleep under the stars.

Then Echo says, "You can stay with us at Mom's." She and Earth are flopping there until after the funeral. They sleep in the same bed where Laura and I made love. The thought gives me the creeps. But she's made the offer. It's hers to make. Laura had made out a will, in which she left everything to Echo. So, when she told me she loved her daughter, she meant every word.

I don't want to stay with Echo. But I accept. I'm a city boy. Roughing it is not my style.

●

I'm in the spare bedroom, likely Echo's room while growing up. Even with a bed and pillows and sheets life isn't easy. There's no electricity, no running water. But Echo's survivalist skills come in handy. She even found a tarpaulin and placed it over the part of the roof the tornado had blown away. She's an able girl. Too bad she has these weird ideas. Too bad there is this gulf between us.

Mostly I stay in my room, the story taking shape on Laura's old Royal manual typewriter which, for some reason, she kept after buying a computer. The tornado swept up my laptop, so it's a godsend. I join Echo and Earth for meals, taken in silence. Otherwise I keep my distance.

After I've succeeded in ignoring her for more than a day she knocks on my door. When I open it she says, "I know how you feel. You've lost someone you loved. So have I. It hurts, Adam. It hurts so bad I can hardly stand it."

"It's hard for me too." I wrap my arms around her, hug her tightly. "It's hard for me too." She clings to me like a small scared child, refuses to let go. So do I. But we do. I ask what her plans are. I want to keep the talk going. I don't know why. It's something that can't be explained. Perhaps I shouldn't try. She says she'll stay here until after the funeral, then return to her place, pick up again.

"So you're staying—"

"Damn right." She purses her lips. Then: "The painting—" (It's still intact, save for some chipping on the frame when it fell from the wall. I pass by it when I leave my room for meals. I'm still struck by its beauty, even more than when I first saw it—oh that seems long ago. Just a couple of weeks, but very long ago.) "—I want you to have it."

I shake my head.

"You don't want it?"

"No."

"Memories, huh?"

Now I nod.

"You may want it later. So think about it."

"Okay. I will."

"But don't take too long. This house's not my style and I plan to sell it. Then the painting will have to go."

"I'll let you know."

"Mom meant a lot to you. You don't want to forget her completely."

"No. I don't."

●

Monday morning dawns bright and cloudless. The service will be in the Catholic cemetery at the northern end of town. Laura asked to be buried there, with her parents and grandparents and great grandparents. She'd written it all on a sheet of paper attached to her will. The Catholic church is long closed, but happily the cemetery remains. Burying Laura in cold hard ground is not how Echo would have done it. She'd have had her body cremated, ashes scattered to the wind. But, good daughter that she is, she honors her mother's wishes.

I'm leaving after the funeral. Tiny will drive me to the regional airport at Epworth. There I begin the first leg of my journey east where I will try to resume a life that probably no longer exists.

Echo is ready. She wears a black dress, one of Laura's. It fits her well. She looks good, pretty: no, beautiful. What's more, her legs are shaved. Ashblond hair is pulled back in a bun, just like Laura when I first saw her, at Tiny's. Pretty eyes set widely apart dance above well sculpted cheekbones. I tell Echo she's the image of her mother, but younger. Then lean over, kiss her forehead. She smiles. It's a good smile. A happy one. I no longer hate her. And she knows.

It's a short walk to the cemetery: two blocks. The casket rests above an open grave. I walk up and place my hand on it, say just two words: "Goodbye, Laura."

●

I'm back east, where I no longer belong. Upon my return I filed my story. It wasn't what the editor wanted and he told me so. "Well, it's the story you're getting," I answered back. He printed it. My chances of another choice assignment are nil. But ask if I care.

Petra is out of my life, has moved on with hers. But Cold River is still in mine. I hear from folks there. Tiny has reopened her restaurant. Her regulars have returned. They will keep her in business for as long as she and they draw breath. Professor Lugenbeel for the moment rents Laura's house from Echo. He says he will rebuild, but he enjoys his temporary digs, very like his old ones, and may end up buying. As for Echo she has returned to her home on the high and lonely plains where she paints from her heart and rears Earth. If Wind is to join him, he—or she— will be sired by another man. We're friends now, Echo and I. She has just written, thanking me again for being there (if too briefly) for her mother. And for her. She needed that, badly. She asks about the painting, what I've decided. I have. It's what Laura would have wanted. And what I want too.

Echo need not ship it. I'm happy to return to Cold River and collect it myself. It will be good to see them all: Echo, Tiny, even Professor Lugenbeel. They will be there. And will be there next year, five years from now. They will stay where they are. It is home.

No Songbirds Are Singing

A waste of time. Really. Tossing stuff into my duffel bag, racing to the spot where taxicabs park. Telling the driver to step on it, else I'll miss my train. And then—

The train is late. Thirty minutes behind schedule. It's supposed to get in at 3.55pm, but the time chalked on the arrival and departure board says 4.25. And it may be later than that. Anybody with a grain of intelligence could have told me Train 36, originating in Atlanta and making all stops in between, never arrives on time. Never has, never will.

This means I'll get into Washington later than I want, may miss the train to Harrisburg and points north. What a crappy way to start out. But start I do. I tell the whitehaired man behind the ticket window I want to go to Washington.

"One way or round trip?" he asks. He wears wide suspenders and his necktie is loose at the collar. His breath reeks of tobacco.

"One way."

One way. That gives me a charge. Take the train and never come back. Good idea. Excellent idea. Best I've come up with. Really.

I've been here six weeks. That may not sound long, but it's six weeks too many: enough time to make me wonder why I came here.

But come here I did, to go to college. Four years of this place, the jerks that populate it. Four frickin years. Thinking about it's enough to drive you insane.

Same thing here. The seats in the waiting room are hard as rock, the room itself mustier than the parlor in Grandmother's house. And she uses it only to receive visitors. People taking the train have use this room every day.

I decide to take a walk. Can't go too far. Train 36 might surprise me and arrive earlier than expected. Miracles do happen. So people say.

To call the neighborhood around the station sketchy is putting it mildly. Hole in the wall lunchrooms, tourist homes with faded signs dangling out front, the liquor store with a handful of shifty looking men hanging around its front door.

I know why they do: something I've learned in six weeks here. You've got to be twentyone to buy liquor and—well, most of us aren't twentyone. We can buy 3.2 beer, but who wants to drink that all the time? So you walk up to one of these men and hand him a ten dollar bill or whatever and tell him to go into the store and buy the hooch you want. When he comes out he doesn't hand you the bottle but instead leads you into a gully behind the store. The gully ends along the railroad tracks just north of where the station platforms end. There you find he's not alone. His buddies jump out from the bushes where they've been crouching. Each asks for his share of the loot. You dole out dollar bills until you're out of money. Then and only then do you get your bottle. You've been rolled.

This hasn't happened to me. But I've heard the stories. They're true. Really.

I approach the store, the men look up. But I walk past them. They return to their loafing and await their next pigeon.

Down the street is an old hotel. Some of the letters on the neon sign touting its name are dark. The rest of the building is just as decrepit: a faded pile of brick once yellow, now dull. On the porch old men sit, gazing at cars passing by. Must be nothing else for them to do, nothing they want to do. None of them notice me. They've been gazing for so long they no longer see what's in front of them.

I turn around, walk past the liquor store where I don't get even a look from the men outside. The train still has not come in. It's still due at 4.25. Good. Or at least as good as can be. I still wish it had arrived on time.

People gather on the platform. Seems I'm the only one waiting to board. The rest are, like me, college men. Unlike me they wait for their dates. This is a party weekend: the height of rush season when the fraternities decide whom they want and don't want.

Among them is my roommate: Lowden Burke, decked out as always in a Harris Tweed jacket and khaki slacks, Repp tie and Bass Weejuns. Why the housing office put us together is beyond me. Really. No two people on this planet are less alike. He sees me, asks why I'm here.

"Going away for the weekend." I'm amazed he asks. We share a room. You'd think we talk, at least sometimes. But until now he hasn't bothered to ask.

"You mean you're not sticking around?"

I shake my head.

"You waiting for Abby?" I ask. She's his girlfriend, attends a nearby women's college. I've met her. She's nice, also quite pretty.

It's his turn to shake his head.

"She can't come," he says.

I ask why not.

"Her aunt's very sick. She had to go home."

"Sorry to hear that." I mean it. I'd like to have seen Abby. "So what brings you here?"

"Pickin up my date."

"Who is she?" I ask, as if I care.

"Friend a mine fixed me up."

"Know anything about her?"

"Nope. And I don't care, just so she's beautiful, stacked like a brick shithouse and humps like a bunny."

I laugh. Hearing him talk you'd think he's the biggest stud ever to grace the first year dorms.

"Yep. Gotta make that impression at the rush parties."

He'll be attending lots of them this weekend. He's in demand. I'm not.

"So why're you buggin out?" he asks.

I have no date, no invitations to rush parties. So, no use sticking around. Really. But I don't tell Lowdie. Don't want to give him the pleasure.

"Decided to go home." I speak the truth. That's where I hope to be—if I make the Harrisburg train. And if I don't? I'll just have to figure that out.

He's about to say something when to the south an airhorn blasts its harsh sound. Around a bend Train 36 appears: two diesel engines, a long string of mail and express cars, and at the end a solitary coach that's beyond grimy. No dining car, no club car, no Pullman cars. Train 36 is the most plebeian of trains: a milk run stopping at every hick crossroads between Atlanta and Washington, places other trains whiz past. It slows down, screeches to a stop. The conductor opens the door and steps off the coach and onto the platform.

People get off, all college girls in McMullen blouses and Pappagallo shoes. One or two wear fraternity pins on their blouses, letting all know they are off limits, some guy's serious steady. Lowdie searches for his date. She sees him first. She's far from pretty: chunky, with thick eyebrows, acne scars.

"Lowdie Burke?" she says in a Deep South accent you can cut with a knife.

Sheepishly he says yes.

"Hi. I'm Molly. Ginny Warner said—"

Lowdie recovers quickly. He always does. Tells her how glad he is to see her, asks how the trip went. Takes her suitcase, hails a cab. But doesn't bother to say goodbye to me, wish me a safe trip. His thoughts are elsewhere: the weekend, the parties, what to do about this dog of a date.

I step up onto the coach, search for seat. That's easy: few passengers are scattered about the car. Up front are two girls my age, maybe a year or two older. In the middle a country woman cradles her baby. A few seats back is another woman, young and ordinary of appearance. Despite Indian summer warmth she wears a heavy coat. A pair of men, yokels, sit in the rear. I take a seat across from the mother, wait for Train 36 to resume its journey.

●

It does, after too much time loading and unloading baggage and mail. Creeps out of the station, gathers speed. Squalid backyards of squalid houses butt against the tracks, ragged children look up from their play, mangy dogs let out yawps: the town presenting its soiled backside to the traveler. Soon we are in the country, on our way to Washington.

But only briefly. After a few miles we stop, at a crossroads: a gravel road crossing the tracks, another paralleling them, a store, a handful of houses. But it has a station—a shack, nothing more—and that's enough for Train 36 to stop.

The next place is more substantial, so the train pauses longer. I look out at pool halls and lunchrooms: businesses that bunch around railroad stations. People are about, almost all men and mostly of the poorer sort. All stay busy at not much of anything. I can't wait for the train to start up, pray there won't be a crossroads a mile or two away. But there is. And Train 36 makes its obligatory stop.

The yokels are engaged in a conversation (if you can call it that) so loud they are heard throughout the car. It's about the wife of a man both know.

"Yup," one of them says, "she's a real piece. Like t' git me some a that."

"Yeah boy," the other says and lets out a laugh that sounds like it comes from a donkey and not a human being. Really.

All this wakens the baby. He lets out a ragged cry. His mother holds him and says softly, "Now hush. Jist hush." She sings a lullaby, one I don't recognize: likely one her mother sang to her. She sings, he cries. If the yokels know what they've done they don't say. They talk and guffaw, the mother can't get her baby back to sleep. And he'd been sleeping so soundly—

Up front one of the girls says to the other, "Gee Jeanie, don't y' ever do anything sides readin them movie magazines?"

"Gotta pass the time, Sherry."

Sherry is peroxide blonde, hair swept up in a beehive, lashes heavy with mascara, cheeks red with rouge. Jeanie by contrast is a quiet brunette with clear skin and pretty eyes.

"Yer lucky," Sherry says. "Y' got them magazines t' read. I aint got nothin t' do 'xcept sit n wait fer this infernal train to git us t' Washington."

Jeanie offers a magazine. Sherry takes a look, hands it back.

"It's all bout Elvis Presley," she says. "I aint innersted in that man."

"I thought ever'body was innersted in him."

"Not me. I could care less bout him. He aint bad enough."

Laughing: "He's bad enough fer me."

"Got an idea," Sherry says.

Jeanie looks up from her magazine.

"How bout we play a game a cards?"

"Sure. Whut y' wanta play?"

"I dunno. Five hunnerd sound good?"

"Yeah. Sounds good t' me."

"On'y problem is y' gotta have four people playin if y' want a good game. But that might not be a problem." Sherry gets up. She has an amazing pair of headlights. And her tight sweater displays them to full advantage. She stands in the aisle and says, "Anybody care t' join us fer a game a five hunnerd?"

The mother has her baby to mind. He's asleep again, she wants to keep him that way. The youngish woman in the heavy coat doesn't say a word. Neither do I. Jeanie's cute and Sherry has fantastic tits, but something in me doesn't want to mix with them. I can't explain it. Maybe it's because I'm in college, they're not.

The yokels answer the call, mosey up front. Introductions are made. Their names are Mack Flower, and Bobby Holder, and they're bound for Washington too. Sherry's glad to meet them and Jeanie seems not to mind.

Sherry flashes a deck of cards. But she lacks a flat surface to put them on. Jeanie—not Sherry, not Mack or Bobby—reaches up to the luggage rack, pulls down her suitcase. It's heavy and she almost drops it. Sherry flips the backs of a pair of coach seats and they sit down to play. The girls face me. Sherry looks hard as nails, but Jeanie? She seems sweet. Genuine. And those eyes: they're big and blue and they're pretty. Really really pretty.

They play and talk, have a good time. The girls do most of the talking, Sherry in particular. Bobby talks some. Mack mostly lets go with that cackle of a laugh. They're having fun. Me? I'm look out the window, not at them. And wonder when we'll get into Washington. Pray the Harrisburg train hasn't left—

●

8.05pm: Train 36 slides to a halt in Union Station. As soon as I can I rush out of the coach, start for the ticket window. I'm stopped by a voice behind me shouting, "Hey mister, kin y' tell me whut track the train fer Baltimore's on?"

She's the young woman in the heavy coat. She is also large with child.

"Haven't got a clue," I say to her and speed through the concourse.

The man behind the window, old and rumpled, offers little hope.

"That train's s'posed to leave at eight o'clock," he says, bored. "You can go see if it's still there, but I seriously doubt it."

"That doesn't do me any good."

"I'm sorry, son."

I doubt he is. But I do as he suggests, race to the gate from which the Harrisburg train departs. When I get there there it is empty.

The man at the gate explains: the train was delayed, just pulled out. I missed it by a hair. If only Train 36 had arrived earlier. If only that woman hadn't stopped me. If only I'd gone right to the gate, not the ticket window. If only—

The next train doesn't leave until tomorrow at seven. That's too late. There must be a way to leave sooner, get to Harrisburg sooner.

So what about the buses? Is one leaving tonight? I could take it, get into Harrisburg in time to catch another bus and—

I stand outside a phone booth. A woman is inside: elderly, white hair and thin face with long bony nose and deep eyes. She talks loudly in a thick accent, reminds me of Mrs Foxman who owns the millinery store back home.

Despite the door, despite her accent, I get what she says. She speaks to her daughter. She's on her way home to New York after visiting another daughter in North Carolina and her train gets in past midnight. She wants someone to meet her. "I don't want to sit all night," she wails. "I don't want to be alone for so long."

A pause, then a smile across that thin face and: "Good, good. I shall see you then. Stay well."

The booth is mine. I call the bus station. A tired voice answers. I ask when the next bus for Harrisburg leaves.

"Seven tomorrow morning," the voice slurs.

"There's nothing earlier?"

"Fraid not."

Damn. I'm stuck for the night. Snatching winks on a bench doesn't cut it, so—what to do? Get a room at one of the hotels across from the station? Costs money. Go back? A possibility. Two trains leave before midnight, will get me there in the wee hours. But that's like admitting defeat. Really.

My stomach growls. I haven't eaten since lunch. And I'm thirsty, not for water, for something stronger. I'm eighteen and in Washington, so I can get it without lying about my age.

I go into the cocktail lounge, take a table. A woman of middle years, ridiculous in a short skirt, comes by. I order an Old Fashioned. That's the cocktail my father always makes. He'd make Old Fashioneds for my mother and himself and when they were finished they would give me the maraschino cherries. That's why I have an Old Fashioned now. It's the only drink I know.

The waitress asks for my ID. I fish it out, show it to her. She looks at it, hands it back without a word. I've passed the test. Figured I would.

I ask if I can get a hamburger. And some fries. She says yes. I sit back, wait for my drink. Soon it comes. I take a sip. Feel very grown up: a moment to savor.

But it ends. Now I'm sitting on a bench, trying with no success to figure out my next move. A well dressed couple sit next to me. They wait for the train to Boston which leaves in about an hour. They like me wonder how to kill time.

"I want a drink," the woman says.

"There's a club car on the train," the man says.

"They won't let us board our sleeper till ten," she says. "That's forty minutes away. Besides you can't get a decent Martini on the train, they're all premixed."

"Do you really need a drink that badly?"

"Yes. I need a drink. I need anything to get off this damn bench."

"They have a bar here in the station."

"What are we waiting for? Let's go."

I'm alone again. No conversations to listen in on, nothing to do but decide: a hotel or a train back to college? Which will it be?

Decisions, decisions. If I don't make one soon I'll be sitting on this bench until seven tomorrow morning. That's one thing I don't want to do.

But what I might end up doing.

•

A voice calls my name: one I know. But now? And here? Is it real?

I turn and there she is: slender, medium height, long honeyblond hair, gentle brown eyes, lips parted slightly. And dressed just right, in McMullen blouse and plaid skirt, circle pin on blouse.

She calls my name again. And I call hers: "Abby?"

Parted lips unfold into a smile.

"Abby, what on earth are you doing here?"

"I was about to ask the same question."

I tell my story. Then: "Lowdie said you went to see your sick aunt."

She laughs. "I lied. Otherwise he'd bug the You Know What out of me, asking why I wasn't coming to see him."

"So why aren't you?"

"I don't want to."

"Really?"

"Yes. Really."

"Well well well. So—where are you going?"

"New York. But right now I'm derailed. Just like you."

She explains. Her train got in late and she missed her connection. Now she must take the same train as the woman who looks like Mrs Foxman. The only difference between her situation and mine is her train originated in Memphis and didn't stop at every hamlet across four states.

"I don't want to spend the night here," she says. "The benches look so uncomfortable."

"Believe me, Abby. They are."

"So why don't we go to a hotel?"

Is she suggesting we spend the night together? Surely not—

"Come on," she says. "It's the only thing to do."

She's not some girl I picked up. She's my roommate's steady. And a nice girl—I think. But I don't want to spend the night on a hard bench. I say yes.

We walk out of the station into crisp October night. Across the plaza neon signs bid us welcome. We choose the hotel that looks the least expensive. Its sign is not as large or as bright, its entrance is not as fancy.

The lobby is a narrow corridor leading to the front desk. On one side is the coffee shop, closed for the night; on the other, the cocktail lounge, still open. A few barflies linger, otherwise the scene is dead as a graveyard at 3am. At the front desk a wrinkled man in a wrinkled brown suit greets us, asks if he can help. His frown suggests otherwise.

"Do you have a room?" I ask, trembling and trying not to show it.

The man eyes me suspiciously.

"I asked if you have a room."

The frown remains. But he says he has one.

"We'll take it."

He pushes a card across the desk. I fill it out, give our names as Mr and Mrs Lowden Burke. I push it back. The man says nothing. I breathe a sigh of relief, Abby smiles. Must be a hotel where questions are seldom asked.

"That'll be five dollars please," he says.

I hand him a five dollar bill.

"There's also tax." He says how much. I reach in my pocket, pull out change and give him that also. In return he hands me a key. It's so worn the name of the hotel is barely legible. I hope it still unlocks the door.

The bellman takes our bags. "This way, please," he says. His uniform is frayed at the cuffs, shiny at the knees, unbuttoned at the collar.

The elevator is a rattletrap. I've never ridden one that moves so slowly—even Train 36 is faster. I swear.

But we reach our floor. The bellman leads us down a hallway, stops at a door in the back of the building. Shows us into the room, places our bags on the floor. I hand him fifty cents. He asks if he can do anything else. I say nothing, but Abby does: "Can you get us a bottle of whiskey, good bourbon? And some ice?"

He says he can. She gives him a ten dollar bill, tells him to keep the change.

"Thank you, ma'am." He leaves to get the whiskey.

"You're full of surprises tonight," I say to her.

"Just thought we'd have a taste."

"I didn't know you drank."

"I've been drinking since I was fifteen."

I shake my head. The night has taken an odd turn; I have no idea what's next. Neither does Abby, but that seems not to worry her.

The room is small and nasty: stale smell of cigarette smoke seeping from every cranny. Worn bedspread, faded upholstery on the chair in the corner. Nicked dresser, soiled curtains, cracked windowshade. Opening the window takes several attempts. Even then it opens only a crack.

"This is so cool," Abby says. "Almost like something out of the movies. I've never been in a place like this."

"Count your blessings." In a room like this back home a man stabbed his wife fifty times and cut her body in pieces. The story made headlines for days. Dad wrote some of them. He's managing editor of the local newspaper, made certain the story was faithfully reported right up until the man's electrocution. That was four years ago and people have not forgotten. I haven't.

"We always stay in the best places," Abby goes on. "Every summer we go to The Homestead for two weeks. Ever heard of it?"

I have. It's somewhere in the mountains of Virginia. Some of my mother's kin have been there. But mostly they go to Eagles Mere. The family has a summer home there, a Queen Anne monstrosity with more porches and bay windows than most houses have rooms. We're from the poor side of the family (newspapers aren't known for paying generously) and our rich relations look down on us. But we go anyway, for a week in August. It costs nothing and we are family too.

"It's real fancy," Abby says. "The men have to dress up for dinner—black tie and all that stuff. We've been going there since, oh my God ever since I can remember. It's a neat place. They've got waiters who carry trays of food on their heads. I'm serious, they do. They carry trays on their heads."

"Do they ever drop them?"

An impish grin crosses her face, followed by yet more impish giggle.

"Once, when I was nine years old. And I was the one that made him do it."

"You little devil—"

"Yeah. He was coming by with the tray on his head and I stuck out my foot and tripped him. You should've seen the food flying in all directions. It was a sight. My parents made me stay in my room for the rest of our stay. I couldn't leave even for meals. They had room service bring food up to me."

A rap on the door: the bellman with the whiskey. I get up and open it. The bellman sets the bottle and the ice bucket on the dresser top, and leaves. I drop cubes of ice into two glasses, pour smooth amber liquid into Abby's glass.

"Tell me when," I say. She lets me pour until the glass is nearly full. I hand it to her, pour half as much into my glass. She downs a goodly snort. Then looks at me with serious eyes. And says, "You don't like Lowdie, do you?"

The girl gets to the point. No beating around the bush for her. I have to say something. Should it be what I really think or what I think she'd like me to think? I don't know. I thought I knew her. But I'm clueless. Absolutely.

I tell her what I think: "Not really."

Oddly, laughter. "I didn't think so. But don't sweat it. I'm not crazy about him either."

She has blown my mind. Really. Blown it to the ceiling. And beyond.

"You mean that?"

"Didn't I just say it?"

"You did. I just find it strange."

She takes another snort: again, a long one.

"It's not strange at all."

"But you're his girl—"

"Yes."

"Shouldn't that mean you like him?"

"Not necessarily."

"So if you don't like him why do you stay with him?"

"Good question." She pauses, then: "I guess it's because that's what I'm supposed to be—his girl."

"Says who?"

"Says everybody. My parents, his parents, the people back home: the ones I grew up with. It's been like that ever since Lowdie and I were going to Miss Foland's dancing class Thursday afternoons after school."

"That's how long you've been together—since dancing class?"

"In a sense, yes."

I drink more whiskey. So does she. And asks me to refill her glass. I do.

"So that makes you his girl—"

"Supposedly."

"But you don't want to be—"

"Not really."

"Have you talked to him?"

"Nope. He wouldn't believe me. He'd say I'm talking nonsense."

That's Lowdie. There have been times when I've tried to explain something and he doesn't understand. It's as if he doesn't want to. Or can't. Either way he doesn't get it. So I've given up, try instead—without success—to accept him as he is: a blockhead. A handsome blockhead, hail fellow well met when he wants to be, but a blockhead none the less.

I used to wonder what Abby saw in him. Couldn't figure it out. Now I do. She doesn't. Yet she remains his girl. Insists she is. Says it in the same breath in which she claims her dislike of him. The girl is a mystery. A big one. Really.

"So what are you doing about it?" I ask.

"I already have."

"You mean when you lied about your aunt?"

"Yeah." She takes a swig, laughs a little. "Wonder if he got himself a date."

"He did," I say and laugh also.

"Hey. What's so funny?"

"I saw her get off the train. You should've seen the look on Lowdie's face."

"She's that bad?"

"Let's say she's nobody's pretty child."

Abby laughs heartily. Meantime I wonder if he's already ditched her. Probably not. For him an ugly date is better than no date.

"He doesn't own me," she says. "Nobody does, except me."

"Mighty independent of you."

"Yeah. But I'm the one who should decide what I do with my life."

"You're going to have to tell him."

"I will."

"When?"

"Don't know. But it probably won't do any good."

"Why not?"

"I told you: he wouldn't understand."

"Did he understand when you told him about your aunt?"

"He didn't tell me not to go see her."

"That's because he couldn't stop you. But what'll you do next time?"

"Maybe there won't be a next time."

"You don't know that."

She shakes her head. "No. I don't."

"So what'll you do if there is one?"

"I'll have to see what happens."

"In other words you're playing it by ear."

"Yeah. Guess I am."

"Just like us. We were both going somewhere. And now we're here. Stuck."

"It hasn't been bad. I mean the talk. We've never done that before, never had the chance. Hey. Can you pour me some more?"

"Haven't you had enough already?"

"No. Not yet."

Reluctantly I pour more whiskey. She wastes no time downing it. A wild look comes over her. Angry. Intense. Determined.

"I'm gonna tell you something: something I haven't told anybody—not even Lowdie."

"Why haven't you?"

"It's something I can't tell him."

"Never?"

"No. Never. Absolutely never." Her voice begins to slur. "But I gotta tell somebody. Gotta get it out. I've kept it inside me too long."

"But why me?"

"Cause I trust you. Can't explain why, but I do. So lemme tell you. Please?"

"Sure."

"Thanks. Something happened, last summer. Something awful that changed everything for me."

"Did it involve Lowdie?"

"Not directly. But yes, it affects him—and how I feel bout him."

"So what was it? What happened?"

She downs the remainder of the whiskey, lets out a belch. And begins: "Some friends and I were going to the beach and we were at one a their houses, getting ready to leave, when I remembered I left something and I went home to get it. When I got inside the house I heard noises. They were coming from Mummy's and Daddy's bedroom. Voices. Daddy was out a town and it was Mummy's afternoon with her ladies' club, so I wondered what was going on. And then I—oh God this is hard for me to say—I saw—I saw Mummy and Lowdie's father in bed together. They were both naked and—and—" She stops.

"Go on."

A second of silence, maybe more. Then: "They—they were screwing. Lord I can't believe I said that. But that's what they were doing. He was screwing my mother. And she was enjoying it. Man was she ever. She was screaming like crazy.

Screaming words I couldn't understand. It was disgusting. Absolutely disgusting." Tears trickle then flow down her face. "Mr Burke screwing Mummy in the same bed she shares with Daddy. It still makes me sick, just thinking bout it."

I go over to side of the bed where she's been sitting and sit alongside her, place my arm around her. "You didn't have to tell me."

"I had to. Had to tell somebody. Ever since it happened it's been growing inside me and it's about to drive me insane. That's why I told you."

She looks at me, whites of her eyes blood red. "Don't you tell Lowdie."

"I won't."

"I don't want him to know."

"My lips are sealed. I promise."

"Thanks."

She smiles. It's a thin one, but at least it's a smile and right now I'm glad to see any kind of smile on her face.

"Question—"

"Yeah?"

"Did your mother see you?"

She nods.

"What did she do?"

"I don't know. I didn't stay around, wanted to get away as fast as I could. But after I got back from the beach Mummy came up and asked me what I saw."

"And?"

"I told her. Then she asked me not to say anything to anyone—you know, bout what I saw. She even asked me to promise I wouldn't."

"Did you?"

Again she nods. "I haven't said a word—till now."

"Does your father have any idea?"

"He's never said anything."

Maybe he knows. If he does will he, like the man in the room that reminds me of the one Abby and I occupy, stab her mother fifty times, chop her body into pieces? No. He's more civilized, not a madman. There may be a divorce, perhaps two. After they're final Mr Burke and Abby's mother may marry. Or maybe not. Yes Abby's father knows and Mrs Burke knows, but neither will say anything. That's how it's done among people like them. It was done in my mother's family. Everybody knew, but never a word was said. Appearances.

Now Abby tells me, "That's why I told Lowdie I couldn't come."

"But you didn't go see your aunt."

"No. I was going to New York. And I still am."

"What's there for you?"

"A friend. She's taking a year off before going to college, living and in New York. Greenwich Village. I'm going to see her, maybe stay a while."

"You're not going back?"

She shakes her head furiously.

"Have you told anybody?"

Again, that mad shake of the head.

"When did you decide?"

"Yesterday morning, after French class. Something snapped." She points to her head. "I knew I had to get away from everything, everyone I've known. Start out in a new direction, in a new place, make a new life."

Wow. I thought I was doing something bold when I decided on a whim to go home. But Abby's light years ahead of me. While visions of kissing off college dance in my head, they remain just that—visions. Abby makes her visions real.

"Are you going to tell your parents, the college?"

"Eventually."

"When, eventually?"

A toss of the shoulder: "When I know who I am and where I'm going."

That shrug, those words said devoid of feeling, dumbfound me.

"They'll worry about you."

"Guess they will. But I don't care. Really."

"You don't mean that—"

"I'm done with that life. Done."

"Does that includes Lowdie?"

Now she nods.

"But you're going to have to—"

"He's gonna know."

But when? And how? She doesn't want to tell him, that's obvious. But somebody has to. He'll to wonder where she is, what she's up to, why she avoids him. He'll want to know if she's all right. He'll ask questions. He may even ask me. And I don't want to answer him.

"Why won't you tell him?" I ask.

"Because—" she begins. And then stops.

"Because—what?"

She doesn't answer.

"You started to say something."

More silence. She looks at me with brown eyes not gentle but sad.

"Tell me, Abby. Tell the truth. Why won't you tell him?"

"Cause he reminds me a his father and Mummy. I wanta forget that."

"You don't have to talk to him. Just write a letter, tell him what you're doing. But you'll have to do something."

Good advice. I'm surprised to be the one giving it. I'm not known for dispensing advice, good or bad. She replies, simply, "I know."

I don't ask what she'll do. She may give another answer that's not an answer. Or, if it is, not the truth.

We've talked for a long time and it's late. Both of us have places to go, trains to catch: mine at 7am. I declare it's time for bed. She doesn't argue.

I let her have the bed, take a stuffed chair that looks none too comfortable. She smiles and says thanks, says it like she means it. Goes in the bathroom, comes out wearing a bathrobe. Pulls down sheets, throws off the robe. Offers a glimpse of a nightgown that's more a slip (and a filmy one at that) before tucking herself in between the sheets. In an instant she's asleep.

It takes me longer. First I must fit myself into the chair. A contortionist would have no easier time. I'm not comfortable: not in the least. But it's the best I can do. After too long a while I join Abby in the land of Nod.

●

Slivers of pale morning light poke through cracks in the shade. My eyes peel open. I try to stretch, bones stiff from being in the same position all night. But I get up, see Abby curled up, still sleeping. Hear her snore, softly. I don't awaken her, instead check my watch. It has stopped. I pick up the phone, ask the front desk for the time. It's 8.13am. Not 8.10 nor 8.15 but 8.13. How precise.

Too precise. And too late. Damn. If only Abby and I hadn't met up. I'd have had to spend the night on a hard bench, catching winks now and then, but I would've made my train. And gotten home.

All that's left is to return to a scene in which my only part is watching others have a good time. Face Lowdie, knowing what I know, resisting the urge to tell. Sink into the misery I've wallowed in since arriving in September. How long ago that seems. How very long ago. Even yesterday morning seems long ago.

Abby stirs. Rolls over from the side on which she'd been sleeping, looks at me with sleepy eyes. "Hi," she says in a voice that's also just woken up.

"Sleep well?" I ask—as if I don't already know.

"Yeah. You?"

"As well as can be expected."

"I'm sorry."

"Don't be."

"What time is it?"

I look at my watch, wound and ticking again. "8.32."

"You missed your train."

"Yeah."

"What're you gonna do?"

"The only thing I can do—go back."

Again she says, "I'm sorry."

And again I say, "Don't be." I don't mean it. But I say it anyway.

"I know you don't want to," she says. "You wanted to go home." And, for a third time, "I'm sorry."

I don't want apologies, I want breakfast. My stomach growls. I ask Abby if she wants some. She says yes, goes into the bathroom. I hear footsteps, water running, taps turned on and off. She emerges, fresh and clean. My ablutions are simpler: slosh water on my face, brush my teeth. Unlike Abby I don't fuss over my looks.

We ride the elevator to the coffee shop. Like the rest of the hotel it's plain, worn out. But it's open and serving breakfast. We choose a table. Although we're the only ones it takes some minutes for the waitress, fat and frowsy, wart on upper lip, to waddle to our table. Abby orders first: orange juice and cinnamon toast. No cinnamon toast, the waitress says. So what about a Danish? They have that. I order two eggs over easy and potatoes and coffee. The waitress waddles off and we're alone. We can talk. Abby begins: "You don't want to go back, right?"

"Do you have to ask that?"

"I just wanted to be sure. So—why don't you come to New York with me?"

I can't believe my ears. Is she actually—

"Yeah. You know, keep me company. It'll be a lot better than going back."

She's right. I'd rather be in New York, with her, than back at college, where I don't want to be, don't belong.

"But you hardly know me—"

"I know you well enough. Know you respect me. So c'mon. It's gonna be great."

Her offer tempts mightily. Visions of Abby and I making our way in the big city rush at me like a wave crashing ashore. Overwhelm, inundate, suck me in. I'm ready to say yes, but instead I say no.

"You mean that?" she says.

"Yes."

"But you want to come with me—"

"Yes. I do. Really. But something tells me not to."

"And you're going to listen to that something—"

"Yes."

"And go back to college and be miserable."

"Yes."

"That's crazy."

"I know. But that's what I'm going to do."

"I don't understand."

"Neither do I."

"But you're doing it anyway—"

"Yes. I have this feeling—"

"What kind of feeling?"

"Just a feeling this may not be a good idea."

"It's a great idea. You don't see me sweating it. So what's with you?"

"There's something holding me back."

"Yeah. Something you can't even describe—"

"But it's there and it's telling me not to go. I'm sorry, Abby. I really want to go with you, you don't know how much I do, but I can't."

Our breakfasts arrive. We eat in silence. I offer to pay for her breakfast. She says no, she'll pay it herself. And she does.

We cross the plaza to Union Station. A train is leaving for New York. I accompany Abby to the gate. A moment remains before she must board.

"Sure you won't come?" she says.

I nod: a sad nod, telegraphing my thoughts.

"Thanks for being a good guy" she says. "You really are." She gives a hug, a kiss on the cheek. Seconds later she is seated by a window, looking out—at me. Smiling. And waving. I smile, wave back. The train pulls away. I keep waving—at nothing. Abby has begun her journey. Now I must end mine.

The next train doesn't leave until late afternoon. I check my duffle bag, walk around Washington. All I can do is think about Abby. And the voice that said no. When the time comes I board my train, find a seat. But don't look out the window. There's nothing I want to see. Really.

The train makes fewer stops than Train 36 and the coaches are cleaner; a dining car is attached. I answer the first call for dinner. A ham sandwich costs more than I usually pay for a full meal. I order one anyway, and a glass of milk. I'm hungry and it's something to do: something to take my mind off the inevitable. Yet I can't stop wondering. Yes wondering what I have done.

●

A half century has gone by and I still wonder: should I have said yes? Then I might have accomplished something.

Pacific Avenue

Spend time on Pacific Avenue and you'll find anything you want. It's all there, all for sale. Fork over three bucks and watch girls dance topless at the Carousel. Go down the street to the Parachute Lounge and for two dollars less listen to a band you've never heard of bang out tunes you know by heart. Walk by a door beneath a sign displaying three balls and buy medals they won't give you on post. You can award yourself a Purple Heart, a Silver Star, even a Medal of Honor, make yourself an expert in any weapon that tickles your fancy. Hand a fin to the bellman at the Ajax Hotel and he will ask if you want company. You'll tell him yes. Spend enough time on Pacific Avenue and you might forget you're in the army.

You can get all this and more any night of the week. But if you really want to scope out the action drop by on Saturday night. That's when the troops swarm into town. Square away your bunk (hospital corners all around, sheets so tight you can drop a quarter on them and it'll bounce), do everything you're ordered to do and do it with a smile and a smart "Yes Drill Sergeant" and come Saturday afternoon you've got yourself a seat on that bus into town.

You jump through hoops for that pass. To get it you see the First Sergeant and to see him you go through Zentmyer. That's Specialist Four Otto Zentmyer and you better call him Specialist or he'll lock your heels, throw away the key.

He can do that. He has that yellow chicken sewn on the upper sleeve of his fatigue shirt and you're a buck private without even a skeeter wing to denote your rank. You want to tell him to stick that chicken up a place where the sun never shines and keep it there. But you know better. After eight weeks of basic, six more of advanced infantry training, you've learned about surviving in this man's army.

"What ya want, Soldier?" Zentmyer bawls like he's the frickin CO.

"I've come to pick up my pass, Specialist," you tell him. You make damn sure to say Specialist: don't and he'll jerk you around even more.

"Yer pass." He squints through specs so thick you wonder how he passed the eye exam. "So you've come to pick up yer pass. What ya done to deserve a pass, Soldier? What makes ya so special? Tell me, Soldier. I'm dyin to hear yer answer."

You stand there biting your tongue while this asshole pulls rank, heaps crap all over you. God knows there are few enough cadres in Bravo Company he can do that to. That's why he beats up on trainees.

It's not like he has it hard: sitting in an office all day, no quicktiming to the rifle range. Off at five, ten minutes later hightailing to the EM Club for a burger and a brew: no mess hall slop for him, thank you. His own room: eight by eight with bare clapboard walls that can't keep out the heat in summer or the cold in winter but affording privacy for him to whip out the latest issue of Playboy for a date with Five Finger Mary. No CQ, no KP, no other details: the Top has seen to that. All he sweats are the levies to Nam. But no problem: he's short, five months and twelve days to go. His chances of slogging through rice paddies are zero to nil.

Zentmyer decides he's tired of locking your heels so he cracks a shiteating grin, says the First Sergeant will see you now. You're lucky that's all he does. When he's really on the rag he'll drop you for pushups for stepping on the carpet in front of his desk, some Mickey Mouse offense like that. That's when you want to strangle the foureyed turd.

The First Sergeant is all business, doesn't look up as he hands you your pass. He's been to Nam, came back with a Purple Heart. Word is he caught friendly fire in the ass. But he's been there. That's more than you can say for Zentmyer.

You zip out of the First Sergeant's office past Zentmyer, who's too busy harassing another Joe to notice you, return to the barracks where you toss your razor and your toothbrush, a fresh change of skivvies and socks into your AWOL bag and double time to the bus stop, hoping to catch the four o'clock into town.

You get there as the bus skids to a halt. Climb on board, drop thirtyfive cents into the till, find a seat, gaze out the window. A basic training company marches past: one hundred sixty trainees herded by drill sergeants nipping at them like dogs at wayward sheep. They sing

> *Sergeant Sergeant hear my plea*
> *All this bullshit's killing me*
> *Sound off one two*

139

Sound off three four
Bring it on down
One two three four one two THREE FOUR

They march past, keeping time lest one of the drill sergeants bawls *"Get in step, bonehead"* so loud eardrums pop louder than champagne corks on New Year's Eve. They march past like ants. Like robots. Four o'clock on a Saturday afternoon (a time when the rest of the nation is watching a game on TV or firing up the grill for some burgers and ribs) and they march, kicking up dust as they sing

GI beans and GI gravy
GI wish I'd joined the navy—

You wonder how they do it. And then you remember: You're one of them. You're out of basic, in AIT now, but you still march in quick time and knock out pushups, crawl on your belly through mud and dirt. Spit shine your boots till you can see your face in them, stand at attention (eyes straight ahead, chin and gut sucked in, heels locked tight) while some punk corporal standing so close to your face you can smell the bacon he ate for breakfast on his breath calls you a queer and your mother a whore. You want to deck him so hard he can't get up. But you're not keen on playing rock hockey either. So you grin and bear it.

That's how you've made it so far. In two weeks you'll be a light weapon infantryman (military occupational specialty Eleven Bravo Ten) qualified to carry an M16 and tote a hundred pounds plus of gear while on patrol deep in a place where the temperature is hot, the action hotter still.

At first you were bound for officer candidate school: twentythree weeks of fun and games at Benning School for Boys. If you made the cut (and not all do) you'd earn the right to let your honey pin second looey's bars on the shoulders of your new officer's Class A uniform, entitling you to pull rank on Zentmyer and all the other asswipes who've made your life hell these last four months.

But after one week in basic you realize all the fancy talk the recruiting sergeant dished out was bullshit. He wasn't out to screw you: like everyone else in the army he was covering his ass. To keep his nine to five Monday through Friday job he had to meet his quota. And to meet his quota he had to sign up guys like you. To do that, he promised you the moon.

And you believed him. Your GPA wasn't good enough for grad school and the draft board was breathing down your neck, so you signed in all the places he told you to. Then you told the women at the draft board to tear up that letter beginning with the word Greetings, you were destined for better things.

That was before you met Lieutenant Crow.

In civilian life he was a cop somewhere in Indiana: Terre Haute comes to mind. And he must have been a fat one, for he sports a double chin and remnants of a paunch even OCS could not sweat off. He can hardly wait to ship out for Nam where his platoon will kill more Charleys than any other unit. He'll make sure they do, make them bring back ears to prove it. Yessir he'll lead one mean fighting machine, toughest roughest sonsofbitches in the entire United States army.

All this he tells to Sergeant Hanks, who's been there with a Purple Heart and two Bronze Stars to prove it.

141

Sergeant Hanks shakes his head. He can't believe what he hears. But Lieutenant Crow doesn't take note. He could care less what Sergeant Hanks thinks. And keeps on talking.

As he marks time in Bravo Company he struts about with a knife tucked into his belt. He's out of uniform but big deal: where he's going they don't sweat stuff like that. They sweat staying alive. And killing Charlie. He knows. To hear him talk you'd think he's Sergeant York and Audie Murphy and John Wayne in Sands of Iwo Jima rolled up into one former cop two months out of Fort Benning.

During breaks in field exercises when many trainees find a tree steal a few z's under, Lieutenant Crow is on the prowl. When he finds a trainee napping he unsheathes his knife. It lands between the trainee's legs, not an inch from his family jewels. The trainee spews a torrent of obscenity. Lieutenant Crow laughs.

Sergeant Hanks watches. And winces.

"He aint gonna last five minutes," he tells Sergeant Gomez. "He's gonna git a bullet in his back and it aint gonna be no VC one either."

Sergeant Gomez nods in agreement.

You've been watching too, listening also to what Sergeant Hanks says. You better take every word to heart. Because if you end up in a rifle company humping through the boonies, men like him and Sergeant Gomez will help you stay alive.

And you're headed there. You'll live longer than Lieutenant Crow and odds are you'll come home alive, but make no mistake: Charley has a bullet with your name on it and your job is to make sure it doesn't find you.

That's why a week or so back when the Old Man lined up the company after breakfast and growled "How many a ya pussies wanta drop OCS?" you were among the first to step forward. The Old Man saw each of you in his office. When your turn came he glared in contempt.

"So ya don't wanta be an officer. That right, Soldier?'"

"Yessir."

He points to the combat infantryman's badge sewn on his shirt above the left pocketflap. And you can't avoid the Big Red One division patch on his shoulder.

"Y'd be giving up and opportunity to serve yer country, build yer character, lead men in combat? I've done that, Soldier. Done that many times. It's like nothing else y'll experience. Ya telling me yer not interested?"

"Yessir."

"What's wrong with ya? Don't ya wanta die fer yer country?"

"No sir."

The Old Man's glare deepened. He wants you to know you're the most miserable, most contemptible microbe of bat shit known to man.

"DisMISSED," he growled in disgust.

You saluted him smartly, executed an about face and quick timed out of the office.

All this is fresh in your mind as the bus lumbers along the fourlane highway lined by beer joints, hock shops, tattoo parlors, cut rate tailors: scummy enterprises reminding you you're passing through the scabby underbelly of an army town. It's fresh because when you backed out of OCS you cut your orders for Nam.

But right now you're on your way to Pacific Avenue. Get there and you can perish those thoughts. For a while anyway.

●

The bus rolls into its gate. You're standing in the aisle, AWOL bag in hand, ready to rush off the bus and out of the station and onto Pacific Avenue with all of its thrills, its delights, its temptations.

Night has yet to fall but already it teems with troops in khakis and Class A greens swarming up and down both sides of the street. Some duck into bars, others pause to gawk into pawnshop windows. Few enter the USO building. Neither do you. You enter the first hotel you see, fork over two dollars and seventyfive cents for a dusty room with a lumpy bed, pegs on the wall to hang your clothes on, rusty water dripping from the taps on the sink. If you want a shower you walk down the hall. It's one step up from a flophouse, but alongside the barracks it's the Ritz. At least you have a room to yourself.

You do not linger. Take a leak, splash water on your face, return to the street. In your mind you devour a thick steak with onion rings on top, fries on the side. But you don't seek a restaurant. Instead you hand three clams to the doorman at the Carousel. He opens a door, lets you enter. Inside a girl in a bikini greets you without a smile, shows you to a table. The drinks are lousy: water flavored with a splash of whiskey. But you're not there for the booze. You're there for the show.

Lights dim: all but the ones around the stage and they're brighter than a sunny day in July. In a pit below the stage a band strikes up raunchy music.

First out is a skinny blonde. Had you not been on post all week, hadn't seen a woman in that time, you wouldn't give her a second look. She's so scrawny her ribcage bursts out of her skin. Strands of stringy hair droop sadly to her shoulders. Her face is neither pretty nor ugly: it's just there. You saw better faces by far at fraternity parties. Every blue moon or so one of those faces belonged to your date.

She calls herself Cherry Pie. No joke: "Hi I'm Cherry Pie," she chirps nervously. She begins dancing, now and then moves to stage's edge so guys can cram dollar bills into her G string. Not many do. She can't dance worth a damn, can't keep time to the music. She's so lousy you wonder how she got the gig.

The buck sergeant at the table next to yours begs to differ. He stands up, waves a wad of bills. Tells Cherry Pie in a loud voice what he wants her to do in exchange for them. She doesn't listen, keeps on bumping and grinding.

"Ya hear me, ya wicked bitch?" Sarge shouts and tells her again.

A bouncer, squat and muscled, grabs him by the arm. "Ya better go, buddy," he says to him.

"Hell no," Sarge shouts and wrestles free, punches the bouncer in the face, sending him to the floor. There's blood on his face. He wipes it off, starts to get up. Sarge gives him a quick kick in the groin. The bouncer howls in pain.

"You bastard," he groans as best he can. "You sonofabitch—"

Sarge kicks him again, this time in the gut. Another bouncer rushes up, lunges at Sarge. He ducks.

Sarge's buddies rally to his defense. It doesn't matter whether they like him. Most likely they don't. But they're not about to let those goons wipe up the floor with one of their own. Fists fly, tables flip over, chairs turn into weapons. Cherry Pie stops dancing. Nobody watches, nobody tucks money into her G string. They're all fighting.

But not you. You duck for cover, squeeze into a corner where you watch Uncle Sam's army reduce the Carousel to rubble. Hear the shrill blow of whistles as MPs and town cops rush in and club heads bloody. You don't want to become a casualty, so you squeeze in more tightly, try to make yourself invisible.

But you're not. Someone is watching: Cherry Pie. She huddles beside you.

You wonder how she got here: wonder also how she found time to put on the raincoat she wears. It's a man's raincoat many sizes too large.

"Ya gotta get me out a here," she says.

You're not sure you can. The front door is on the far side of the room. You could try to weave through the melee, but chances are you won't make it.

"I know another way," Cherry Pie says. "Come with me. Please. I don't wanta be alone."

You follow her to a side door not far away. Everybody's too busy fighting to see the two of you slip outside.

On the street you become part of the crowd. That's because you look like everyone else: Joe Trainee enjoying a night on civilian streets. But not Cherry Pie. The raincoat scrapes the sidewalk, its sleeves hang inches past her fingertips. She sticks out like—you get the picture.

"Got anything on underneath?" you ask.

She shakes her head. "Just my G string. My clothes're all back in the dressin room."

"Can you go back and get them?"

"The cops. I can't let 'em see me."

You don't ask why. You may not like the answer.

Cherry Pie's hands fumble around in the pockets of the raincoat.

"Shit." (Her voice mixes anger with frustration and fear.) "My pocketbook, my keys: they're all back there. I can't get in my place if I don't have my keys."

"Then you better go back."

"I told you—I can't."

She wants to get as far away from the Carousel as she can. So do you. And you're hungry: not for Cherry Pie but for some honest chow.

"I'm going to get something to eat," you tell her. "Like to join me?"

She says yes. She knows you no better than you know her, maybe less. But she'll take a chance. Anything (it seems) beats going back to the Carousel.

Down the block is a greasy spoon that's so greasy you can't see through the windows. You go in anyway: you and Cherry Pie. Nobody will ask why she wears an overlarge raincoat though it hasn't rained all evening.

You spot a rear booth and take it, open a menu that's greasier than the windows and study it. Behind the counter a cook (fat with stubble on his chin, heartshaped tattoo on his arm) fries up a sweat. It drips from his brow to the grill where it sizzles along with burgers and bacon and eggs and whatever else he's got cooking.

A waitress as fat as the cook, orange hair so thin you can see scalp, brings two glasses of water and sets them down. There's not a chip of ice in either glass.

"Whut's it gonna be, kids?" she asks, bored.

Cherry Pie orders a burger and a Coke. You go for scrambled eggs and homefries, toast and coffee: hardly the steak dinner you promised yourself.

"Hey I forgot t' say thanks," she says after the waitress has left.

"Glad to do it." Then: "All right. Why won't you go back to the club?"

She crumples her paper napkin, begins tearing it into pieces. "Promise ya won't tell?"

You nod. She keeps on tearing.

"I ran away from home. If the cops find me they're gonna send me back."

"And you don't want to go—"

"No way."

And you think you're in a world of hurt. Cherry Pie's in so deep she's about to sink into it. You want to know how she got there, how she plans to get out.

But you don't ask. She may not answer and if she does it may not be the truth. She's been lying for so long her life has become a lie. Take her name: Cherry Pie. You want to know her real name. But again you don't ask.

You stare into her eyes, a sad shade of pale, and wonder why she left home, how she ended up at the Carousel. Wonder how she keeps her body together (but not her soul: you're not sure she has one). Wonder about things you don't know, questions she won't answer. Wonder also why you're sitting with her in this ptomaine parlor, not in a nicer place wolfing down that thick juicy steak, those crisp fried onion rings: sitting by your lonesome, no complications dogging you.

But instead you're stuck with Cherry Pie.

You gobble your eggs, she picks at her burger. By the time you're finished she's still picking. You wish she'd hurry up, wander off to wherever it is she plans to go. But she hasn't planned. She'll cling to you until something better comes along. And what will that be? Your guess is as good as hers.

A thought occurs, one that—try though you might—you cannot put out of mind. You say to her: "You don't have a place to sleep, right?"

She says no, for once tells the truth. So you'll take with you. You cannot refuse her. Something in you— something that existed before the army began reshaping you, something you won't let it take from you—compels you to help.

"Ready?" you ask.

She looks up. A chunk of hamburger remains on her plate, a piece of bun too, but she lets them be. You're ready to leave and that means she is too.

In your room Cherry Pie unbuttons the raincoat and drapes it over the chair. She stands before you, makes want her. Want her now.

First you ask, "How old are you? And tell the truth."

She gulps, stares downward, does not look up to face you.

"Sixteen," she says.

That's jailbait. But in light feebly cast by the bare ceiling bulb she tempts. Does she ever. Fondles her breasts, slowly moves her hands down her belly, just as slowly peels off her G string. The striptease arouses you. You try not to let it show. For she's underage: off limits.

But also a woman. She bleeds monthly, can bear children, make milk in those nubs of breasts. She's a woman in every way that counts and right now she looks good even though she's skin and bones and not very pretty and you don't like her and balling her could land you behind bars.

"C'mon," she says. "Lemme show ya the things I can do."

She's good, very good. Knows the moves, knows like she's done them for years. And she's only sixteen.

You pull a cigarette from the pack on the nightstand.

"Can I have one?" she asks.

"Sure."

She lights up off your cigarette, takes a drag. I say to her, "I'm curious about something."

She looks at me, says nothing.

"Why'd you leave home? You don't have to tell me if you don't want to."

I don't expect her to answer. But: "Yeah. I'll tell ya. Ya deserve t' know." Then: "It was my brother. Stepbrother actually: He's my stepfather's son by his first wife. Well, I was standin in my room lookin at myself in the mirror n I didn't have any clothes on when all of a sudden I heard this sound. It was Raymond standin in the doorway. Stupid me, I forgot t' shut the door n he walked by n seen me. Well, there was nothin I could do t' stop him. When he was done he looked at me real ugly and said 'Little girl, ya say one word n I'll kill ya.' And I b'lieved him. Soon's he went away I packed some stuff n split. I been on my own ever since, getting by any way I can." She stubs her cigarette. "Now ya know why I can't let the cops find me." Then she snuggles close. "Put yer arm round me. Please. I want ya t' hold me. Yeah. Hold me tight."

You wrap your left arm over her shoulder. Your fingers touch a breast. She doesn't push them away.

Soon she's asleep. You follow. Not even the bright lights, the teeming sidewalks, the unceasing noise of Pacific Avenue can awaken you.

●

You know it's morning because gray light floods the room forcing you to face the day. No signs flash outside your window, scarcely a sound breaks the calm. It's Sunday morning and Pacific Avenue sleeps off its drunk.

The other side of the bed is empty. Cherry Pie has gone. She must have crept out while you were sleeping. You shouldn't be surprised. She lives by her wits, landing gigs in topless bars if she's lucky, turning tricks if she's not. But you, friend, are bound for the rice paddies. You'll come home with a chest full of medals if you're lucky, zipped up in a body bag if you're not. You may be worse off than Cherry Pie. At least she won't be sweating a VC bullet.

You're not due back at Bravo Company for another eight hours. But the bars are closed, the lights switched off. Though it's Sunday morning not a steeple is in sight. But you're in no mood for a sermon. All that's left is to catch the bus back to post. You wash, shave, begin dressing. When you look inside your wallet, to see how much money is there, you find none.

She took it all. The dirty little whore: she let you ball her, told that sob story about her stepbrother—told it so well you believed every word—and while you were sleeping she rolled you. No wonder she was gone when you woke up.

You finish dressing and round up your gear, race down the stairs—not the elevator: it's too slow—and ask the man behind the glass window if he's seen a skinny blonde in a raincoat that's ten sizes too large.

He shakes his head. But you have feeling that even if he'd seen her he wouldn't tell you.

Now you're really up Shit Creek. You have no money for breakfast, not even thirtyfive cents for busfare.

You walk along Pacific Avenue, hold out your thumb. It's against regs, but you have no choice. Soon you get a ride. You're on your way back to post and, sometime later, off to war. You keep hoping somehow you won't go. But you're hoping against hope.

You sit in silence as Pacific Avenue slides past, try not to look. You want to forget about it, even more forget about Cherry Pie, now probably halfway to her next stop. You've seen the last of her. And if you're wise you've also seen the last of Pacific Avenue.

Time

Not a dead ringer, but close. Same long light brown hair, now plaited in a thick braid reaching below her waist. Same eyes, big and blue and sparkling. Same smile, wide and natural. Same clear skin, same small and slender build. Not beautiful, not sexy. But very pretty.

She stands at the hostess stand by the door, in white blouse, scarf of many colors around her neck, black pants, sensible shoes. The sight of her stuns me.

"You're my first customer," she says, still smiling after forty years.

I smile back. "I am?"

"Yeah. Like I usually don't get one the exact moment I open."

A difference: never before has she inserted "like" into sentences at random.

"Well, here I am." Another difference: making talk was easier then.

"And I'm glad you are." She laughs, same nice laugh, and scoops up a menu, shows me to a table by a picture window looking out on a patio. Somewhere beyond, blocked by a row of palm trees, is the ocean.

"Julio will be your server. Hope you enjoy."

I tell her I will. Her smile doesn't go away. It never has—

—She was Holly then. Now she's Kaitlyn. That's what her nametag says. I don't know where Holly is. Whether she's married, divorced, has children, grandchildren. It's as though she's vanished from the earth.

Until six thirty this morning when I saw this girl who calls herself Kaitlyn.

Julio stops by, asks if everything's good. I say yes. But I lie. I cannot focus on my food. All I think of is Holly, in my thoughts again. But has she ever gone away? No. Never entirely.

I try to finish my breakfast. There's a meeting to attend and I must have sustenance. But I'd rather sit here, watch Kaitlyn, think of Holly. Of how it seems only yesterday when last I saw her.

I sign the chit, add a twenty percent tip. That's what is left these days. In college we didn't tip, we were too poor. There were no credit cards, we lived on what our parents sent us. Happily there was a beanery where meat, potatoes, vegetable, roll and butter, dessert, coffee could be had for ninety cents. Nowadays that won't cover half the sales tax. But then it bought a full meal. And no tip.

Enough of this. Time to go to my room, prepare for the meeting. As I leave Kaitlyn/Holly beams, asks how things were. I beam back, tell her they were fine. But there's one thing: the time. I'm not used to getting up when I usually do and it's four in the morning, not seven.

Laughter ripples, stirs more memories.

"That's when I gotta get up."

"You get up at four?"

"Every day I'm working."

I ask why.

"I live like fifty miles away and I gotta be here to open up."

"At least the freeways aren't crowded."

"Yeah. And I get off at like two thirty and they're not busy then either."

"And the rest of the day is yours."

"Yeah. That's good."

"I'm still not used to it, the time difference."

"How long're you here?"

"Till Thursday."

"Y' oughta be used to it by then."

"Just as I'll be leaving." A pause. "Say, have you been east?"

"Once. I went to Washington."

"Did you notice the time difference?"

"Did I ever. When I got up it was like wow I must've overslept."

"Just like when I got up and thought I hadn't slept long enough."

A man and a woman appear. Kaitlyn—or is she Holly?—grabs a menu, seats them. But not before smiling at me—

—The meeting is as I feared: a bore. I don't want to be here. Don't want to look at the guy across from me, his $3,000 suit, $400 haircut. He has nothing to say, just sits smug and superior, lets all know he's doing a favor by being here. I've known my share of jerks, but he defines the word.

I tune him out. Drop out of the meeting. Turn on to *San Francisco, January 14, 1967. Out of college, soon to enter the army. Went west for a final fling. Spent last night in North Beach, checking the topless scene. Even got a topless shoeshine. Crappy shine, but the girl's tits were okay. Hit too many bars (two drink minimum at each one), by some miracle got back to my hotel on Union Square. Come to at noon, ask the lady at the hotel newsstand what's happening. She says it's at Golden Gate Park. The Human Be-In. A Gathering of the Tribes. All the bands: Jefferson Airplane. The Grateful Dead. Big Brother and the Holding Company. Name the group, it'll be there. I begin walking. Halfway there a hooker who must weigh three hundred pounds asks if I want a date. I don't. At last I reach Golden Gate Park, look out on twenty thousand people jammed into the polo grounds, jammed close, tripping, grooving to the sounds. Quicksilver Messenger Service takes the stage. Twenty thousand people, all ages, all colors, all sexes, one purpose blend without effort into a multicolored One, tripping, grooving. Gig ended, Quicksilver exits, a man with unkempt gray hair and turtleneck and love beads comes on: Dr Timothy Leary. Psychologist. Writer. Guru. He stands center stage, hurls words: "Tune in, turn on, drop out." They cheer, those twenty thousand trippers, groovers. Tune in. Turn on. Trip eight miles high, soar into space. A moment in time,* a small piece of history. They didn't know it then. Neither did I. It didn't sink in until years later, *at a cocktail party. I'm talking with a couple, friends of a friend. The wife's from San Francisco, born and bred. I tell of my visit. Tell of the Human Be-In. Her eyes light up. "Hey I was there too,"* she says. She'd read about it in the *Chronicle* and went. She was fourteen years old. I ask what she told her mother. She laughs. "*But we're still alive, you and I," I say to her.* "Good point," *she says. Many of those twenty thousand are no longer around. They tuned in, turned on. Dropped out, dropped dead. But we're here. That's something. Yes* and for what? To be at a meeting I don't want to attend, sitting across from a man I can't stand, thinking not of Here but Then. Not where I am but where I've been, what I've done, wishing I wasn't Here, was still back Then. God how I wish I was back Then, anywhere but Here.

The jerk deigns to ask a question. I tune in, trip from Then to Here, give an answer. The words slip from my mouth. I have no idea what they are. But they must be the right ones, for he smiles, insincerely. I tune out, trip back, from unhappy Here to happier Then. It wasn't always happy, I know. Sometimes I wished I wasn't living Then. But now, Here, it's a time I recall fondly. A time I wish I could return to. But can't.

I check my watch. Eleven o'clock. Another hour until lunch. Until I can see Kaitlyn, think of Holly. Think of Then that wasn't always happy but has become so. Yes think of Then, anything but Here. Think of Holly. Of how she got away. And didn't come back. Until now—

—Kaitlyn gives me a good table, again by the picture window looking out at the ocean I can't see for the palm trees.

"Must be rough, driving fifty miles to work, fifty miles back," I say to her.

"Yeah. Gets tiring."

"And expensive." I've heard about gas prices here. Everyone has.

"Least it's not gonna be much longer. I'm moving, first of the month."

I ask where. It's the city next over. She can't afford to live here. Few can. This is a cocoon for rich people who don't want to be famous, just rich. Very rich.

"That should make it easier," I say.

"Will it ever. Like I won't have to get up at four. One thing though."

"What?"

"The rent. I gotta pay like a thousand dollars a month for a one bedroom apartment. No frills. Nothing. Not even a pool."

"I pay about half that for two bedrooms."

Her jaw drops, pretty blue eyes look to pop from their sockets.

"But it's nothing special. That's my fault."

She asks how.

"I haven't made it special. The woman across the hall has. Her apartment's special. Mine isn't."

Now she asks why.

"Because I've never made it a home. A place to sleep in? Yes. A place to do my work in? Yes. But a home? Never did that."

She asks why not.

"I just never did. But you? You'll make your apartment a home. Doesn't matter how drab, how ordinary it is. You'll do that, make it a home."

"You think?"

"I know."

The wonderful smile unfolds. "Oh that's so sweet—" She looks over, sees people waiting to be seated. "Gotta go. We'll talk later."

I hope we do—

—She entered my life three years after I left the army. I was on my second job: a time when I could quit work on a Friday, toss my belongings—clothes, books, stereo, everything—into the back of my car, and start a new job first thing on Monday. Pick up and leave, hoping to seek a new life in a new place. But each time it wasn't a life I found, only an existence.

We were thrown together *at this newspaper in a city that's the largest in that part of the state but not the state's largest. I'm on the copydesk, editing stories written by others. She's a news clerk, taking obituaries, doing scut work. It's a crap job. But she's new in town and this is the job she found.*

She and I both work nights, five nights a week. We sit alongside each other, on the state and local desk. She's cute: big blue eyes, brown hair falling below her shoulders, freckled nose, great smile. Natural, nice as can be. When I have no copy to edit, she's not taking obits or running errands, we talk. At first we talk a little. Then we talk more. After a while we talk a lot.

"*So you're from Seattle,*" *I say during a break. We're allowed two breaks. One is to eat: thirty minutes, hardly time to down a meal. The other is ten minutes. This is the ten minute break. We're in the employee lounge, the only ones there.*

She nods.

"*I've been there.*"

Her eyes light up. "*You have?*"

"*Yeah. I took advanced army training at Fort Lewis.*"

"*That's wild.*"

"*And when I had a pass I'd skip Tacoma, head for Seattle.*"

"*Good move. Tacoma's a bummer. There is no there there.*"

"*Gertrude Stein.*"

"*Huh?*"

"*She wrote that.*"

"*Yeah. One of my professors in college said it was one of the best sentences ever written.*"

"*It's not just one of the best, it is the best. Five words and one of those words used three different ways. But she wasn't writing about Tacoma. She was writing about Oakland California. She went back to the neighborhood she grew up in but it was gone. Torn down. There was no there there."*

"Wow. I don't remember my professor saying that. But it does fit Tacoma. I've never seen any there there."

"Oh there is there there: pawnshops, bars, lots of bars, places soldiers like to go to. But not this one. I went on to Seattle."

"Don't blame you. It's a neat place, neatest there is."

"So why did you leave?"

"Wanted to see more of the country."

"But why here?" There is there here but there is more there elsewhere.

"My sister moved here, year ago. Thought I'd come and stay with her."

The break is over. End of conversation. But we pick it up later.

"How did your sister end up here?" I ask.

"Her husband's company transferred her. You know how that goes."

I do. But with me it's getting tired of living somewhere, moving someplace else. Call it mobility. Not upward. Not downward. Just mobility.

"Do they like it here?"

"Yeah. Least they say they do."

"How about you? You like it here?"

"It's different. But yes. I think I do."

"You like it well enough to want to stay here?"

"I don't know. Do you?"

"Do I—what?"

"Do you like it here?"

The answer is no. I didn't like the last place either. I hope I'll like the next one. And there will be a next one. But I don't say that. I just shrug—

—One night after work we go out together. At that hour you look for a place that's open all night, feeding people who don't work the same hours most folks do. But not us. We're hungry for talk, not food. A hot steamy restaurant packed with people is no place for that. Instead we go to a cocktail lounge just off an interstate ramp. I order Jack Daniel's Black Label with water. She has one of those fancy drinks women go for. After the waitress brings our drinks we get into talking.

"You really don't like it here, do you?" she says.

"It pays the bills."

"That all?"

I nod. "Isn't it the same for you?"

"Not quite. It's something I haven't done before. That makes it interesting. At least for now."

"But later?"

"I might think like you. But I'm not there yet."

"What'll you do when you get there?"

"Find something else, I guess. Now—what about you? What turns you on?"

"Writing."

"So why don't you become a reporter? They write."

"But not what I like to write."

"And what's that?"

"Fiction. Stories that come from my mind, not off a police blotter."

"Have you written any?"

"Some."

"Have you published any of them?"

"Not yet."

"Why not?"

"They're not as good as I want them to be."

"Maybe they'll never be that good."

"But that doesn't mean I should stop trying."

"Will you let me read them—you know, when they're good enough?"

"Sure."

"Thanks. I love to read. And I'd love to read your stories."

"You'll be the first. I promise."

She says nothing, just smiles. But that smile tells me everything.

We finish our drinks. I signal the waitress. She brings the check. I place a ten dollar bill on top, tell her to keep the change.

"But it's only six dollars," she says.

"Keep it anyway."

"That was generous," Holly says.

"I'm in a generous mood. It's been good, us sitting here."

"Yeah. It has—"

—Once or twice a week after work we head here. It's noplace special, but we like it. It's where we can talk. I order my Jack Black. She orders her drink that has a name I can't remember. The drinks get no better. But the talk does. One night I mention the Human Be-In.

"You were there?" she says.

I say yes.

"What was it like?"

I tell that also. Tell how I had witnessed history but didn't know it then.

"Did you hear Janis Joplin?"

"She wasn't on while I was there."

"I loved her. Loved how she belted out a song. She put all her heart into it. It was a tragedy when she died. She and Jimi Hendrix and Jim Morrison."

"I did hear Timothy Leary though."

Her eyes pop wide open. "You did?"

"Yep. Heard him say 'Tune in, turn on, drop out.' First time he said it."

"Wow. That's so cool. So you actually heard him?"

"With my own ears."

"Man you were there. You saw it happen."

"It was one of those things."

We talk more, of other things, until closing time. Holly goes to her sister's place, I to my apartment where I sleep, shave and shower, and nothing more—

—Holly sips on her drink and says, "I'm leaving."

I say nothing. I'm too stunned. After a space I ask, "Where're you going?"

"Back home."

"Don't you like it here?"

"It's okay. But I want to go back. You understand, don't you?"

I do. And I don't. I understand she may be homesick. What I don't understand is why so soon. She hasn't been here two months.

"I'll miss you," I say. "It's been great, being with you."

"And I'll miss you too. I'll miss you a lot. You're a great guy, a great friend. Yeah I'm sure going to miss you. And I won't forget you. Won't forget the time we've had. But—" (a smile, sad) "—it's time for me to go home."

Must be a guy. Something happened: an argument, a bad one. She came east to get away. But they've worked it out and *she's going back to him. She needn't say a word. Probably doesn't want to. And I don't want to know. Better to preserve memories. The truth might destroy them.*

Hold it, buddy. Your imagination's working overtime. Maybe she does want to go home. And that's all.

I take her at her word. That's enough.

"You'll keep in touch, won't you?" I say.

"Sure will. In fact you can even come out and see me."

"You mean that?"

"Wouldn't have said it if I didn't. I'd love to see you."

"It's a deal. I'll be there. I promise—"

—But I never went. I wrote to her, she wrote back. I intended to write again but never found the time. A few months later I changed jobs, moved away, continued along the road to my present job, editing instruction manuals. And unlike the other jobs I've stayed at this one. I'm at an age when I have run out of places to go.

Other women have come in and out of my life. One even married and divorced me. I can say more about them than I can say about Holly. But none has lingered like she has—

—It's my final day in the cocoon. Not once have I turned on the TV, looked at a newspaper. I'm as detached from the world as the people who live here. Not like people living in the world: people who drive, some for miles, to work here. People like Kaitlyn. Yes Kaitlyn. Likely she knows nothing of Gertrude Stein. Doesn't know what "There is no there there" is about. Has never heard of the Human Be-In, has never listened to Janis Joplin. It's not her fault. She was born too late in time. She's just a sweet kid who reminds me of Holly. Of what might have been, if only I had kept in touch—

—I continued to write stories. I didn't write them for others. I wrote them for myself, wrote what I wanted to write in ways I wanted to write. Over the years I'd written a stack of them. And when I was done I wouldn't read them. They gathered dust on a shelf in the room where I do my work.

One day I took them down, began reading. A sufficient number were good enough to collect into a volume I published a couple of years ago. People bought copies, not many but enough for me to claim a readership. The book made almost no money. But it did justify the years I spent, writing.

Wherever I go I bring books with me: never know when someone might want one. Nobody at this meeting did. They're not people who read fiction. They read what they think is useful. Fiction isn't useful. So it didn't hurt my feelings when none of them bought my book. I never expected them to.

But there's someone I want to read it. On this last day upon finishing breakfast I go to my room and fish a book from my suitcase, write a little note on the flyleaf. Return to the restaurant where Kaitlyn stands poised to greet people. I hand her the book.

"Is this for me?" she says.

I say it is and explain: "You remind me of a girl I knew, years ago. She got away from me, but I still think about her. So I want you to have this book. I want you to remember who I am and why I gave this to you."

She thanks me. Not once, not twice, but many times. She thanks me until she runs out of ways of saying it. Then she says, "Oh I love to read. I just love to read. I know I'm gonna love reading this book."

Words Holly said, years ago. She said she loved to read, would love to read my stories. I wouldn't let her. But now I let Kaitlyn read them. I even give her a book so she can.

And I hope she will read them, enjoy them. Hope they'll help her remember me as I will remember her. Just as I remember Holly. And always will.